ALFIE, DARLING

EFFIE CAMPBELL

Oh sweet Alfie is in for quite a ride... as are you dear reader! Enjoy a walk on the unhinged side

Love,
Effie Campbell

Editing by Katie Awdas of Spice Me Up Editing

For those who have ever thought - I'm not worthy of that kind of love.
You are.
Enjoy this downright, dirty tale of healing trauma and feminine rage, but beware; you might need to avoid lasagne for a little while...

This book contains spicy content, depictions of death, torture and sexual assault. There are copious unhinged intimate scenes. There is vivid torture and violence toward and by main characters as part of the plot. Consent isn't always explicit.

It is also written in the UK, and I use British English for spelling. If you are from elsewhere - forgive me! Remember that these are hot Scots and just imagine it in their voices, it makes it all better.

ONE

ALFIE

Another hopeless date.

Another night with blue balls.

Another night of having to return to the McGowan mansion and see Ewen, my long-time family friend, eating up his new squeeze. I'd seen enough of the two of them to know he was falling hard and fast. Despite the giant house, it was feeling real small, thanks to their impassioned sex games and near constant swooning.

They didn't even invite me to play.

Rude.

A drizzle began, sending droplets bouncing off my blazer and causing my hair to stick to my face. Dinner with the McGowan clan awaited, but being surrounded by the bevy of heart-eyed couples made me shudder. It was the last thing I needed.

Warm orange light and upbeat music poured out of a pub as a group of giggling women tumbled out onto the street. A waft of sweet-smelling perfume followed them like a cloud of candy floss. It should be criminal for women to be so damn addictive—my biggest weakness.

Glancing at my watch, I paused before heading into the pub.

One drink couldn't hurt. Ten minutes, and I'd be on my way.

Inside, people bustled in every available space. Seats held more than one patron as groups squished in together. A pretty red-headed woman, face full of freckles and lips that were sinfully plump, filled the small stage in the corner of the room, singing a country song full of sass. Confidence exuded from her, filling me with warmth. There was nothing I loved more than a woman who knew what she wanted. Her eyes flicked from patron to patron, drinking down their admiration like a little attention vampire.

After a few minutes, the barman got me a pint, which I sipped slowly while watching the singer. Her eyes met mine with a glint that spoke entirely of trouble. Placing my pint down with a smirk, I took off my jacket and hung it over my arm before folding up the sleeves of my shirt. She ate up every second of it, actually licking her lips as I revealed my tattooed forearms.

One pint turned into three while I waited for her set to end, enjoying the little game of cat and mouse we played. Time was running away with me. The McGowan's were likely too busy to miss me much anyway.

'Ladies and gents, I'm going to take a quick ten-minute break before coming back for the second half of my set.' She winked before blowing a kiss to the crowd.

The busy pub cheered as she stepped down from the stage, her eyes razor-focused on me.

'I've not seen you here before,' she said, grabbing the pint from my hand to take a generous sip and handing it back to me. Brazen. Hot.

'You've got a little foam,' I commented, reaching out and wiping the beer foam from her upper lip. She captured my wrist and drew my thumb to her mouth. I couldn't help but groan as she licked it off, her tongue wrapping my finger. A shiver of desire surged through my chest, an insatiable craving I couldn't help but chase again and again. Bed to bed, person to person—no matter how many legs I fell between, it was never enough.

'I've only got ten minutes,' she whispered, dropping my hand and leaning in close, filling my nose with her floral perfume. My lips grazed the side of her neck just below her ear as I closed my eyes and indulged in her heady scent.

'Not enough time,' I murmured, pushing a hand into her hair and tipping her head roughly.

She squeaked, sending a thrill right down to my dick, leaving me straining against my pants. Her eyes widened, and her breath hitched, her voice dropping an octave when she spoke. 'I could show you what else I can do with my tongue.'

Dinner could wait another ten minutes. Right?

'Where?' I demanded.

She grabbed my hand and led me through the crowd, past the bar, and into a tiny corridor. Pushing her back against the wall, I slid my mouth over hers, unable to fight back the wave of hunger that swept over me. Whether ten minutes or a night, knowing someone wanted me gave me the rush I craved. The rush I couldn't resist. She whimpered into my mouth when I grasped her by the ass and pulled her tightly against me, our bodies crushing as I drank down her eager kisses.

She broke the kiss first, panting against me. 'I want to suck your cock. I've only got a few minutes left until I need to be back on stage.'

'And what if I want to use my tongue to make you scream?' Nothing was sweeter than a woman going to pieces beneath me.

'Then you'll have to come back and visit. I'm here every Saturday. Now shut up, and let me have what I want.'

Dropping to her knees, she undid my trousers and pulled my cock free, her eyes glittering at the deliciousness of a random hook up. The hubbub of the busy bar filtered through the space, reminding me just how close we were to them. Such a dirty girl, ready and willing to suck a stranger's dick at the drop of a hat.

Just my type.

'Jesus Christ,' she said, taking in the ladder of metal that graced my erection. Her eyes swept to my face as she reverently leaned forward and traced her tongue along the series of piercings before surrounding the tip with her pink lips.

'No, sweetheart,' I said, my eyes closing as I rested my head back against the cool wall. The familiar sense of calm filling me while I dove into the distraction of desire. 'It's Alfie.'

By the time I made it to the sprawling stone mansion where Ewen lived I was most definitely late for dinner. The home wasn't mine, but felt like it was. It was the place I resided most whenever I was in Glasgow.

The five McGowan siblings and their partners gathered around the elongated wooden dining table, different takeouts littering the surface. Sometimes I could pretend I was one of them— another brother, instead of being alone in the world.

Sure, I had my hedonistic pleasure castle in the Highlands, which provided me with plenty of distractions. I had my loyal staff members, like Grieves, who were always there and steadfast. I had a syndicate I profited from, but I delegated leadership responsibilities to others after my father's passing.

What my life lacked was people who were mine. No sisters and brothers. No parents left. Just my lonely self stumbling from party to party, indulging in whatever I craved, but without ever having people who wanted me to be there without it being about my dick.

Chatter bubbled amongst everyone around me as they ate, and I took a breath, steeling my shoulders and applying the usual mask I wore in front of others. Maeve, one of the McGowan siblings, was speaking about not letting her now-adult adopted children into their uncle's club when I walked into the room.

'Yeah, right,' I said, grabbing a slice of pizza before taking a seat. 'You two just want to get it on in public, I bet.'

Maeve rolled her eyes but fixed me with a beaming smile as her husband, Cam, let out an exasperated, 'Alfie.'

All gazes turned to me, watching as I bit into the lukewarm pizza. The salty, cheesy taste hit my tongue. Delicious.

'Where've you been?' Ewen asked.

'Had a date.' The less info, the better. The date had been a disaster anyway. Finding myself in the singer's mouth had been a silver lining, at least.

The conversation continued, and they swept me up in their easy sense of belonging. I ate and listened, picturing myself as part of their family. But no matter how welcoming they were, the reality remained unchanged: they weren't truly mine. I should have married one of the two sisters while they were single. Wed my way into their circle. Maybe Logan, the eldest of the clan, and his wife, Valentina, would welcome a third into their marriage? They had already welcomed me into their bed...

Reaching out, I picked up my wineglass and refocused on the ongoing conversation. Katie, Mac McGowan's wife, was grilling Ewen and his paramour, Cora, about what was going on between them. Poor Cora had really been thrown in the deep end. She was a sweet woman who must have been feeling as alien as I amongst the tornado that was the McGowan clan.

'She's swept him off his feet,' I said before lifting the glass to my lips and taking a sip. My eyes widened in surprise as the wine burned its way down my throat, leaving a bitter taste in its wake. 'Fuck me, what is this shit?'

Around us, everyone burst into laughter. Cora released a breath as the attention diverted from her. She gave me a thankful smile when I winked at her.

'It's the first batch,' Logan said, his cheeks reddening. 'Lessons were learned.'

When Ewen leaned in close to Cora's ear and her entire body melted against him, jealousy bubbled up inside me.

I hated it.

TWO

HARRIET

So close.

Alfie walked ahead of us, dodging through the people who had spilled out of the noisy pub to our right. Raindrops speckled my cheeks like fine freckles as I gained on him. We had to catch up to him by the alley, or we'd miss our chance to grab him.

'Not so fast,' Petros hissed under his breath. 'We don't want him spotting us.'

Blood stormed through my veins as I grew closer to him—close enough to smell his spiced aftershave. My nerves were singing from being so near to finally having him, so I was caught entirely off guard when he stopped in front of me.

Petros caught me around the waist and pressed me against the wet wall of the pub, his body neatly engulfing mine right as Alfie turned. With his hand cupping my jaw, Petros leaned in close to my face, his breath mingling with mine. To all the world, it would appear that we were lovers so caught up with one another that we had to steal a kiss right there in the rain.

'Don't let him get away,' I whispered, the warmth from Petros' chest sending a wave of emotion through me.

Desire.

Guilt.

Shame.

Petros' dark eyes swept my face, his expression as neutral as ever.

Within a breath, Alfie had pivoted in his tracks and walked into the commotion of the pub.

God damnit.

Petros stepped back, leaving the cold air to fill the gulf between us.

'How is he always so fucking unpredictable?' I asked.

'Either sheer dumb luck or some sort of god is on his side. We can try again another night.'

'No.' The word came out in an angry spurt. 'I'm going in.'

'Harriet...'

Petros knew damn well that I did what I pleased, and he had the choice to either follow me or stay behind. As always, his footsteps clipped behind me as I made for the door.

The bar was packed with people, intoxicated and brimming with mirth. Bodies swayed to the music of the singer performing on stage, while others flirted, hoping to avoid going home alone.

Where the hell was Alfie?

Scanning the room for his shock of dark hair, tension bubbled up inside me.

'There,' Petros said, nodding over to the very end of the bar, behind a group of lads clad in green football shirts.

There indeed.

Up to his usual tricks, making eyes at the red-headed singer who was lapping up his attention. She had no fucking idea what a good-for-nothing nepo dickhead he was.

Spoiled.

Rotten.

My blood pressure soared with each minute I stood idly, waiting for Alfie to leave. I discreetly used my phone camera to take a picture of him from behind while he stared at the vocalist, swiftly tucking it back into my pocket.

'You can't just stand there, shooting eye daggers into the back of his skull.' Petros pushed a glass into my hand that I didn't bother even looking at. He knew I wouldn't take a drink in a bar.

One drink had ruined my entire life.

The condensation-clad glass was cold against my tightly gripped fingers.

'We need to look inconspicuous,' Petros whispered near my ear, his voice fighting the way through my rage as it so often did. 'Need to be unmemorable.'

My breath shuddered in my chest as I inhaled slowly, trying to replace the white-hot anger with an ounce of Petros' calm.

When the music stopped some minutes later, the singer walked up to Alfie, lust leaking from her when he leaned in and spoke to her.

With my heart in my throat, I wanted to walk over and slap some sense into her, but she wrapped her tongue around his finger before following him to a door near the back of the room.

'Let's just grab him,' I said, heading towards the door that Alfie and the redhead had disappeared through.

'We can't, there are too many witnesses here.' Petros caught my wrist and gave me a pleading look. My eyes went from him back to the peeling, flyer covered door.

We were so close.

'He needs to pay. I'm sick of waiting. He's probably in there fucking that singer as if he's done nothing wrong. Every orgasm the asshole has is one too many.'

Petros hand slid down to catch my fingers, his solid calmness filtering through his touch. 'You've waited twenty years for this, Harriet. Striking wrong could mean losing your chance for good. A few more days won't hurt. He needs to disappear without a trace.'

With a sigh, I dropped his hand. Petros was right. He was almost always right. The soft breeze to my tempest, reeling me in when it wasn't yet time to unleash.

But boy, I would unleash on Alfie Rosenhall when I had the chance. He was going to hell on earth before I sent him down there for eternity.

'We'll wait for him to come out, and then get him into the van in the alley,' I said, placing the still full glass down on a nearby table. Pulling out my phone, I snapped off a few pictures of the bar.

The singer emerged a little time later, her lipstick smudged, and her hair mussed. From across the room, I could tell her eyes were dilated, her body languid.

It made me sick.

I photographed her, too. You could never tell what would come in handy.

'Where is he?' I said, my eyes dragging back to the door.

'I'll go look,' Petros said.

He disappeared through the door, only to reappear a moment later, his shoulders bunched in agitation.

Making my way towards the front door, I met him there.

'Gone. There's a rear entrance. I think it must lead out to the alley.'

I was out of the door, tumbling into the street, looking wildly around the busy road.

A mass of dark hair ducked into a taxi, the door closing swiftly behind him.

'Fuck,' I cursed, kicking out at the wall as the car moved off.

Petros stared after the vehicle, his dark brows pulled downwards in a scowl. 'We'll get him, I promise.'

My chest rose in angry puffs as the car's lights disappeared around a corner.

Enough was enough.

'No more sneaking around. I'm going to use the one thing Alfie can't seem to resist.'

Though, the very thought of it made my stomach turn.

'Harriet.' Petros' voice twisted with tortured pity. 'You can't.'

'Everyone else has used my body for their gain. Why shouldn't I?'

Turning on my heel, I made for the van.

Filled with fury.

And determination.

THREE

ALFIE

The barman topped up my glass of red while I looked at my phone for the twentieth time in half an hour.

After a week of teasing me on the dating app, I was convinced she'd show up.

Pulling my collar out from the back of my neck, I adjusted myself on the bar stool, taking another look around the room. The hotel reeked of wealth, its marble floors stretching in every direction, reflecting the splendour of the enormous overhead chandeliers.

Vixen.

That was the name she'd given me. A taunting little vixen indeed.

'I'm sure she'll show,' the barman said, giving me a hopeful smile. He probably meant well, but it was like another little stab of the knife to my sense of self worth. This was why I didn't date. Random hookups or meeting people at my hedonistic resort were safe. Easy. The desire was raw and readable. Fuck, what if it wasn't even her messaging me? What if it was Mac or Logan fucking with me? It would be just like the McGowan boys to pull my leg like that. A smile stole over my mouth. I wouldn't mind being the butt of their pranks, it would be like being one of them.

Logan's fortieth party would be starting in less than an hour, and as much as I wanted to celebrate with them all, it was going to be happy couple central. I'd been hoping to lose myself inside my dating app friend for a few hours first.

The pianist's music filled the room, weaving in and out of the low hum of conversation around me.

My phone screen remained entirely void of any life.

Sighing, I gathered up my phone and rose from the bar stool.

'Leaving so soon?' A husky voice caressed over me, and I turned towards it.

God damn.

A little taller than me, she stood gracefully in heels that made her legs seemingly miles long. I felt weak at the very sight of her. Her shoulder-length blonde hair cascaded in sultry waves around her face, tempting me to run my fingers through it.. Full lips dominated her captivating features while her alluring hazel eyes, fixed on me, gleamed with excitement.

'Thought you'd decided not to meet me,' I said, leaning forward to air kiss each of her cheeks. She shivered at my closeness, and I grinned. Pent up already huh?

'Hopefully I'm worth waiting for,' she said, her words lightly accented with a northern English accent. Maybe Manchester?

'I don't doubt it for a moment.'

We both sat down, her tanned legs crossing over and leaving her sharp black heel grazing my trouser leg. The slight touch was enough to ignite me with promise.

'Can I get you something to drink?' I asked.

'A glass of champagne, please.'

The barman readied our drinks while she practically ate me up with her gaze. A confident woman ready to take what she needed was the hottest thing going. I liked to take the lead as much as any man, but being looked at like a tasty morsel by a self-assured woman made my knees quake. She looked like she'd give as good as she got.

'So, Vixen, do I get a real name yet?'

'What's to say that's not my name?' She took the glass of bubbling champagne but didn't lift it to her lips.

'Were your parents hippies?' I joked, flashing her a grin.

A tiny flash of darkness flitted through her face. Shit. I was only kidding.

'No. They were not. You haven't earned my name.'

Shifting myself to face her, I set my knees either side of her legs and looked fully into her eyes. 'Pray tell, how do I earn such a reward?'

'I'm sure we can find something you're useful for.' Her teeth grazed her lower lip while she looked at me through her long lashes.

We must have been similar ages, both nearing forty. Not the usual type who wanted anything to do with my hedonistic lifestyle. I tended to attract those looking to explore, looking for one hot night. She looked like she could snap her fingers and have men eating out of her palm.

'I do like to be useful.' I lowered my voice while drinking her in. She moved the toe of her heel, lightly stroking against my leg. Little tease. The bartender smirked to himself before giving us a bit of space, moving down the bar to busy himself with some glassware. 'Tell me, Vixen, what is it you're looking for tonight?'

Her throat bobbed as she swallowed while setting her gaze directly on me. 'Just one night to remember.'

The turn of phrase was an odd choice, but the spark that lit up her face, the hunger she could barely conceal, told me I was in for one epic night.

'And you think I'm the man to deliver?'

'I know you are,' she said with a smirk, leaning forward to give me a delectable view down her dress.

In the confined space of the elevator, energy vibrated between us, hinting at the delectable sexual tension that would erupt the moment we got behind closed doors. My fingers twitched by my sides, wanting to reach out and graze the flesh at the hem of her dress. Stepping closer to her, I inhaled her sweetly perfumed scent, smiling at our reflection in the mirrored doors. Tipping her head ever so slightly made her blonde waves fall from her neck, leaving the expanse of olive skin exposed.

I couldn't resist.

Moving forward, I grazed my lips over the spot below her ear, satisfaction rumbling through me as she shivered. Just as I moved to envelop her in my arms, the lift pinged, and she walked towards the opening doors. I followed her down the carpeted hallway to her room. The lock chirped at a swipe of her key card, and then we were inside. Floor-to-ceiling windows gave a view over the Glasgow cityscape, and the suite was luxuriously decorated in dark, golden tones.

'Nice room,' I said, shucking off my jacket and hanging it neatly over the back of a chair. The living space had a series of leather sofas, a kitchenette and dining area. Vixen picked up a remote control, flicking a music channel onto the TV and pumping up the volume.

'Mmm, looking to be extra noisy tonight?' I said, moving towards her before wrapping my arms about her waist and pulling her to me.

'No fun in the silence,' she replied, her kohl lined eyes meeting mine.

One of my hands skated up over her dress, and I cupped her chin, tipping her mouth to mine, desperate for a taste of her.

Before I could capture her lips, she diverted my mouth to her throat. 'I don't like kissing.'

Swallowing down the disappointment, I pressed my lips against the hot skin of her neck, pouring my need against her beating pulse. I fucking loved kissing. The heat, the passion, the driving intimacy. It wasn't unusual for playmates to avoid it, particularly if they were a couple, but every time it left me feeling unworthy. Good enough to fuck, but at arm's length.

Focusing on the way her heartbeat quickened against my lips, I nipped and sucked my way along her collarbone. Her fingers tucked into my hair, directing my mouth to where she wanted it.

A dull vibrating noise broke through my concentration.

'Sorry,' she said breathlessly. 'I'll just get that.'

Grabbing her phone from her purse, she gave an apologetic smile before ducking into what I assumed was the main bedroom.

To pass the awkward moment alone, I admired the artwork on the walls of the living room before moving towards a series of doors. A quick freshen up wouldn't go amiss. The drinks from the bar were already sitting heavy.

Opening the first revealed a small cupboard holding an ironing board and other bits and pieces.

The second was a dark room. Reaching around the doorway, I found a light switch and flicked it on. Bright light illuminated a small, messy bedroom. Takeaway containers littered the desk along with multiple abandoned paper coffee cups. A pair of man's boots lay discarded against the end of the bed. It didn't line up with the neatly put together Vixen here for a one-night stand at all.

My brow creased. Was it one of those family rooms which were adjoined? Had the hotel left the wrong door unlocked?

A reflection in the desk mirror caught my eye. Photographs and pieces of paper were stuck all over the wall behind the door. I walked into the room, letting the door close behind me as I focused on the images.

The McGowan mansion, but from afar.

Me walking down the street on the phone.

The pretty red-headed singer with her mouth wrapped around my dick.

What the fuck?

There were dozens of photos spanning back over weeks. Sweat pricked at the back of my neck while my eyes went from picture to picture, trying to absorb the information.

Vixen was *stalking* me?

With a shudder, I grabbed a handful of the photos and shoved them in my pocket, hoping they'd be useful in finding out who the hell the little psycho was somehow. I needed to get out of the room first though.

Pulling the door ajar, I peeked out. The main living area was still empty. Thank God. Her call must have been taking a while. My body screamed with the wrongness of being there as I made my way to the exit, knowing I just had to get downstairs to the front desk. With my breaths sounding deafening with each step, I glanced over at the other bedroom door, praying it remained shut. While I could probably give as good as I got if she attacked me, I'd much rather let the police deal with her. If she was mad enough to stalk me, track me down online and lure me there, what else would she be capable of doing? Did she have a weapon?

My palms slicked with sweat as I reached for the door.

Almost there...

'Alfie?' Her voice was still low and sultry. Securing my hand on the handle, I looked over my shoulder and gave what I hoped was a convincing smile.

'Just going to fetch us some champagne.'

'No need. There's plenty in the mini bar.' A steeliness entered her voice.

I pressed down on the handle, but it didn't budge. Some sort of contraption was fitted around it, preventing my efforts to open the door. I clawed at the obstacle in frustration, yet it refused to move.

Fuck.

Turning around, I lifted my chin in defiance.

'Let me out of here,' I demanded.

'Oh, Alfie, darling. I don't think so.'

'Why the fuck have you been watching me? Who are you?'

'Maybe if you'd have asked me that twenty years ago, we wouldn't be here.' Her eyes sparkled as she slid a hand up her thigh, tucking it beneath her dress and retrieving a hidden knife from a sheath strapped to her leg.

'What do you want? Money?'

She laughed, a high, tinkling laugh that made my stomach turn to jelly.

'No. I don't need your money. Far too little, far too late.'

She was closing the space between us step-by-step. I didn't want to hurt her, psycho or not, but I'd be left with little choice.

'Put the knife away, and let's talk this over. There has to be something I can give you in exchange for letting this go.'

The knife twirled in her fingers as she licked her lips. 'You're going to give me everything I want, Alfie. Including your very last breath.'

I didn't wait for her to come closer, I rushed at her, hoping to incapacitate her long enough to call the front desk and have them send backup. I'd avoid the police if I could, but if they had to be involved, then so be it.

Her eyes widened at my sudden movement before our bodies collided. I'd expected her to crumple easily, but she was solid muscle beneath the pretty dress. We tumbled to the floor, air whooshing from her as I tried to avoid the jabbing of her knife.

Flipping us over, I pinned her underneath me, my thighs gripping her waist. Using one arm to pin her knife-wielding hand, the other fought to capture her other.

'I don't want to hurt you,' I grunted as she fought like a hellion.

'Fuck you,' she said, her mouth turning up in an amused grin. A nervousness snaked along my spine at her expression. I had her pinned. Why did she still look so unfazed?

A loud crack sent a blinding pain shooting through my skull, knocking me sideways and clean off her. The ground met me with another blistering crack, my body rendered useless, dizziness making my vision swim. My chest constricted as the throbbing spasms in my head bloomed to an overwhelming ache.

A set of men's shoes came into view from where I lay unable to move. A hand reaching down, helping my stalker to her feet. The heels clicked against the floor, the noise making my head ache more with each strike.

Crouching beside me, she took a vial and needle from the man, tipping it up and filling the syringe with a colourless liquid.

Laying there while she pierced the needle into my neck, I could do nothing to defend myself. Entirely at her mercy.

Fuck.

'See you soon, Alfie,' she whispered, pressing the plunger down and sending a nipping pain into the injection site.

I tried to fight it.

I tried.

I failed.

FOUR

PETROS

Cursing as his shoes caught on the edge of the large cage, I dragged an unconscious Alfie through the entrance to his prison.

The fucker was heavier than he looked.

The sedative would be running out soon, so I had to work quickly to strip him down to his underwear, fitting the heavy shackles around his ankles and wrists. Long chains sent clanking through the space and into the decadent room beyond. Harriet had installed the cage in her entertaining space the previous year, but Alfie was its first inhabitant. A sliver of jealousy snaked through me at the intense obsession she had with the dickhead.

Perhaps when he was finally dead, she'd be able to move on. We both could.

Seeing him tortured would hopefully bring her the answers and peace that I couldn't.

With a grunt, I threw Alfie's shoes and trousers out of the cage area before stopping to look down at him.

Dark tattoos whorled across his chest, arms and back, a mixture of patterns and mandalas. His chest rose steadily enough that he didn't seem to be in any danger of dying from the knock to the head nor the heavy sedative.

Unfortunately.

I'd sooner have seen him die.

Swallowing down the jealous anger that bubbled into my throat, I shook my head. Harriet needed the closure only he could bring. I'd seen what she'd suffered at the hands of men like Alfie and his father. Whatever she needed, I'd help her achieve it.

The cage door closed with a loud bang, making Alfie stir briefly before his body resumed its limp state on the floor. Satisfaction flooded me as I locked the door, sealing him inside. We'd disposed of his phone after switching it off at the hotel. His friends could probably track him there, but after that, they'd be screwed.

We didn't exist.

I'd been stolen and smuggled into the UK as a child. Harriet was presumed dead.

Even as her alter ego, her existence was in question. A rumour discounted by anyone who was anyone.

But she was real.

And soon enough, she'd leave a bloody path that would make her existence impossible to deny.

They'd whisper her name in fear instead of jest.

And I'd be behind her every step of the way.

Making my way through the rust-worn tunnels that connected our warren, I sought Harriet out. Being away from her pained me. If I was with her, I could make sure she was safe. Make up for all the times when I had to stand idly by as they hurt her. Had to listen to her begging for help while standing by, my soul dying with every tear.

Never again.

She may not feel for me with the intensity that I adored her, but I could be there to protect her for the rest of my days.

Women loitered in the tunnels, some moving from one area to another, others chatting or sitting alone. Harriet and I had taken over the disused bunkers when we had to flee, slowly working to make it a safe haven for women like her. A place where they could come to start again or receive help to return to the lives they were ripped from. Men being there was far rarer. There were a few trusted souls other than I who aided us in our endeavours. All knew that one wrong move would prove fatal. Harriet was unrelenting in her goal to eradicate abusers. None would survive under her roof.

Soft humming met me as I opened the door to our private space. We'd been roommates for years, and returning to her filled me with as much joy as it did torture me.

Her blonde hair fell in waves around her face, skimming her shoulders while she stirred something in an old mixing bowl. Flour dusted one cheekbone, and when she looked up at me, her small smile swept me away. No matter how restrained Harriet was, she held me captive with nothing but a look.

'Is our guest all settled in?' she asked, tipping the bowl so the batter slid down into a baking tray.

'I guess you could say that. He's still out cold.'

'Good.'

She placed the mixing bowl on the counter, and I leaned forward, swiping a finger through the batter.

'No!' she shouted, making me jump. Darting forward, she slapped my hand away from my mouth before I could taste it.

I paused, staring down at the sticky brown batter still clinging to my finger as realisation set in. 'Who are the cakes for?'

Harriet passed me a cloth and grinned. 'They're muffins.'

'Mhm. Laced with poison?'

'Only a little.'

Moving to the sink, I washed my hands thoroughly to remove any remnants that might cling to my skin. 'Who are they for?'

'Mick Johns.'

'Harriet!' I said, exasperation filling my voice. 'He's an MP, you can't poison him.'

'All the more reason. He was abusing his wife. He deserves it.'

'They'll suspect her, you'll put her in more danger.'

Harriet's eyes narrowed. 'They can't. She's dead. He killed her, and it's being swept under the rug because of who he is.'

The muscles in my jaw tightened at her words. 'How do you know?'

'The coroner is a friend of Nancy's. He told her that the wife came to him in a hell of a state. Bruised. Broken. He wasn't the one assigned to her, but he helped with her autopsy. He's sick of seeing people turning a blind eye.'

'So, you're just going to walk up and give him muffins? He'd be an idiot to accept them.'

Harriet placed the muffin tin into the oven, and turned to face me, a wicked smile stealing over her face. 'It's his birthday tomorrow. One of his buddies is sending him a pretty escort to play with, to cheer him up after his wife's death. Just so happens that we've intercepted that request, and we will be sending one of our own women in her stead.'

'What if he hurts her?'

'He won't get the chance. His buddy ordered the muffins to contain something to give his friend an extra boost. From what I hear, he's struggling more these days in that department. It's a shame he wasn't more specific.'

My beautiful terror. Dissuading her would be impossible. Vengeance was what she lived for. Hers, and for all the people who couldn't seek it.

I only wished I could find a way through her granite exterior and give her more reason to live. To make her happy.

'So, what's the plan with Alfie?'

Harriet leaned back against the oven, her tongue briefly sweeping her lower lip in a way that made me want to go trace its path with my own. 'We make our little caged bird sing.'

'How?'

'Everyone has a weakness, we just need to find the right one to exploit. I doubt money will work; he has plenty of that. Pain, perhaps. Threaten the people he loves. We'll find the crack and prise it open until he gives us the information we need.'

I folded my arms over my chest, watching her thoroughly clean the mixing bowl and spoon before putting it into a bin bag. Another one for the incinerator.

Letting my thoughts wander, I pictured us in a different life. In a proper home, not stuck below ground living as society's rejects. Being able to come into a room and sweep her into my arms. For the muffins to be edible. To have her all to myself without our crushing pasts. Would finally getting revenge on the right people allow her to accept kindness and love? I had it oozing from every pore, and it was all for her.

But she didn't want it.

Not yet.

Maybe not ever.

FIVE

ALFIE

A deep heaviness tugged at my wrist as I tried to roll over. Cold seeped into my back, the skin feeling like I'd been lying on ice.

'What the hell?' I mumbled, forcing my aching eyes open.

The ceiling above wasn't the one at the McGowan mansion, nor my room at home. Curved dark metal met at an apex above me, my eyes taking in the riveted edges. Following the edge of the wall downwards brought my eyes to a series of floor-to-ceiling bars. Bars which separated me from a decadently furnished room. The large, green leather sofas wouldn't have looked out of place in my hedonistic castle. What were they doing in whatever this place was? A groan escaped as I pulled myself to sitting, taking in the thick metal bands that were locked about my wrists and ankles. Chains snaked away from me before disappearing into the floor. Lifting my arms was a workout in itself with the weight of the thick metal bonds.

Waking up nearly naked and in chains wasn't exactly unusual for me, but it usually came with a night of decadent fun. All I had were chilled bones, a thumping head and confusion.

The cage extended the width of the room, and there were no windows on either side of the bars.

What was this place? Some sort of upcycled farm building? Why was I there?

The pretty blonde flashed into my head.

The syringe.

The photographs.

Shit.

I must have really fucked her off somehow. But how? Generally, people didn't take a captive for failing to phone back after a hook up.

She was likely just the pawn. There had been a man there. The blonde must have been a honey trap.

Damn me and my needy fucking cock.

Storming towards the door, dragging my heavy chains behind me, I felt a hard tug. I didn't have enough give to reach the barred door. Pulling hard enough to cord the muscles in my arms proved useless. Cursing, I gave it another try, the harsh metal shackles cutting into the skin of my wrists. True terror clawed at me as the reality of the situation gripped me.

Taking a breath to calm the torrent of panic that roiled in my stomach, I closed my eyes and focused on returning my heart rate to a normal pace. Fear and panic never served anyone well.

Whoever it was likely wanted money. I could get that to them without a problem. If it wasn't money, they probably needed a job taken care of or a favour from someone like the McGowan family. Either could be discussed and resolved.

It would be fine.

Probably.

Sometime later, after I'd dragged myself to sitting on the edge of the bare mattress in the corner, footsteps approached.

The man who walked towards me was tall and had that deep olive tone of the Mediterranean. I'd have said that he was attractive if it weren't for the absolutely sour look on his face.

'Ah, about time,' I said, trying to keep my voice light. 'I'm sure we can figure out a solution to whatever the problem is. I won't take it to heart that you've treated me less like a man and more like an animal.'

He stopped by the sofa, crossed his arms, and ignored me entirely.

'It will be much easier to chat if you could get me my clothes and let me out of here. We can sit down man-to-man and stop all of this.' I signalled to my surroundings. He didn't even look at me.

'The silent treatment is very immature, you know.'

Nothing.

I was losing the will to live with him by the time another set of footsteps came clacking along the solid stone flooring.

Lighter steps.

Glancing up, she came into view. The lying little vixen. Seeing her coming towards me in jeans and a sweatshirt while I was in nothing but underpants left me feeling vulnerable. She closed the space between us, coming to stand next to the bars.

'You did this?' I asked.

'No, Alfie. *You* did this.'

'And what am I supposed to have done?'

Her eyes practically gleamed in the low light of the room. 'I'm sure you'll figure it out.'

'I don't even know you. Is this because I fucked you at some point and never called?'

Her sharp laugh cracked through the space. 'You think far too highly of yourself.'

'So, what is it? Money? How much do you need? Let me go, and I can have it in your account within the hour.' My elbows dug into my knees from sitting on the edge of the mattress, trying to keep my body language open. Non-threatening.

'I don't want your money.' Leaning her body against the bars, she grinned at me, sending warning flags soaring in my head.

'What do you want?'

'Information.'

'That's it? On what?' I asked.

'On your father's depraved group of perverts. I need names.'

My brow creased at her words, what was she talking about? 'My father is dead.'

'Indeed. I'm quite pissed that I wasn't the one to see him take his final breaths. Still, his associates are likely very much alive. I need their names.'

His business associates were all public knowledge. It couldn't have been them that she meant. She'd said perverts, did she mean Rosenhall?

'Rosenhall is a club. The people there might be classed as perverts to some, but they are all there because they choose to be. Safety is a priority of mine.'

She looked at me as though I was an idiot, rolling her eyes.

'I'm not talking about your little club, Alfie. You know what I'm talking about, and playing dumb won't save you. I'll have those names out of you one way or another. The longer you hold out, the less intact you'll be when you die.'

Ah. That little slip was all I needed. She meant to kill me with or without the information I didn't possess. My best hope was to hold out until someone found me. But would anyone even look for me? While I lived part time with Ewen McGowan in the city, it wasn't unusual for me to go off on an adventure for a few weeks at a time.

Shit.

My own unreliable lifestyle would be my fucking down fall.

I was going to have to try and smooth talk my way out.

Somehow.

'You may as well kill me now,' I said, hoping bluster might work.

'Don't tempt me with a good time,' she replied.

'You wish.'

Her jaw ticked at my words, clearly having some effect on her. Hopefully not a murderous one.

Her manfriend, servant, boyfriend? Whatever he was, he stood by in the background intently watching her talk to me. Most henchmen at least tried to look uninterested in the goings on around them. He was focused on her like a hawk.

Would he be a weak point to exploit? Or an obstacle?

Either way, I was entirely at their mercy.

SIX

HARRIET

Even the sight of his stupid smug face filled me with rage.

What I wanted to do was to storm into his cage and make him suffer. To pour all of my years of anger into a thousand cuts on his tattooed chest.

Sitting on one of the sofas, I half listened to the chatter around me as the room filled. A mixture of excitement and nerves was palpable in the air. The club room where Alfie had been detained was always busy on an evening, but especially so at the weekend. Women and men we'd helped knew it was a safe space they could come to with people who understood what they'd been through.

The half-naked man in the cage was a bit of a talking point.

'Gosh, he's covered in tattoos,' Nancy, one of my few longer-term friends, said.

'He's a creep,' I responded, taking a sip of my drink.

'Are you sure?' Her gaze lingered on where he lay on the mattress, facing straight upward, utterly ignoring the goings on. 'He doesn't really look that threatening.'

'You know as well as I do that creeps can be as attractive as they can be repulsive. Someone's appearance doesn't make them good or bad.'

'I know. I just don't get that feeling from him. His aura isn't giving that off at all.' Nancy shrugged.

Honest to God, Nancy and her bloody auras. While I couldn't deny she was often pretty accurate in her character assessments, I didn't believe in glowing hazes or whatever she claimed to see. And I *knew* Alfie was a piece of shit.

A piece of shit who was looking *far* too comfortable.

'Take him out,' I said to Petros, who hesitated for a few seconds before prising the keys from his pocket and unlocking the cage.

Alfie didn't put up a fight as Petros pulled his hands behind his back and fitted a set of handcuffs to his wrists before removing the heavy shackles. Seeing Petros manhandle Alfie gave me an uncomfortable tingle low in my stomach. One I pushed away, unwilling to explore it.

Petros walked Alfie out of the cage and towards me. Eyes all around watched with interest as Alfie held his head high, not seeming the slightest bit fazed by the fact he wore nothing but boxer briefs in a room full of clothed people.

His lack of shame made me see red.

Petros forced Alfie down to his knees a few feet away from me, and the way Alfie met my eyes left me unsettled. He should have been fearful. Should have cowered.

He didn't.

Inky tattoos covered the majority of his chest, stomach, arms and neck. A mixture of different artwork that spoke of decades beneath the needle. No stranger to a bit of pain then.

'Are you ready to tell me what you know?' I asked, sitting forward and resting my elbows on my knees.

'I've as little to tell you now as I had earlier.' Even his words were confident. Cocky little fuck.

'This room is full of people who would love to see you bleed, Alfie. They'd love nothing more than for me to push you to the ground and sever your pathetic dick from your body. To listen to you cry and scream and beg. Being a cocky cunt isn't your best course of action here.'

The fucker bit his lip to try to hide the smirk that lifted the edge of his mouth. Worse, his cock pressed thickly against the material of his underwear.

'Oh my God,' Nancy breathed beside me.

Was he... turned on by this?

'What the fuck is that?' I asked, my words laced with disgust.

Alfie looked down before shrugging.

Rage filled my limbs as I stood and pulled my flick knife from my pocket, barrelling down on Alfie and kicking him to the floor. He landed with a grunt, his back squashing his bound arms between him and the floor.

'You repulse me,' I said, pinning him beneath my shoe, the sole digging into his throat. 'You should be begging for your fucking life, and instead, you dare to get turned on? To make this about your dick. Just another abusive fuck like your father.'

Alfie groaned, his throat bobbing beneath my shoe.

'I can't help it. If you are going to threaten me with a good time, my dick's going to join the party.'

Leaning down, I slipped my knife between his hip and the fabric of his boxer briefs, severing the material and letting it fall from him.

A collective gasp arose at his exposed cock. Which only made me all the angrier.

But I understood why. Silver gleamed along the veiny shaft, a whole ladder of piercings. Fucking hell.

'I should do you a favour and cut it off if you can't control it,' I said, unable to drag my eyes from his throbbing, studded erection.

'It works better when attached if you need to borrow it so badly.'

My muscles bunched at the very idea. Grinding my shoe down on his neck, I cut off his air, watching him as he tried to pretend like it didn't affect him. Soon enough, he writhed beneath my foot, his face reddening as he fought for a breath. Putting more weight on my leg, I smiled.

'If you keep being a mouthy fuck, I'm going to get a pair of pliers and tear every one of those piercings out one by fucking one. No one here cares whether you live or die, Alfie. Your use is extremely limited, and I will find a way to get what I need out of you. One way or another. Your cunt of a dad is dead; stop protecting him and his friends. Is it worth suffering for them?'

His eyes fluttered as his legs twitched, and I took my foot off his throat, letting him gulp down desperate breaths. I would enjoy seeing him take his final breath soon enough. For now, I needed him alive.

His cock was even harder than before.

I raised my eyebrows as he coughed and heaved on the floor. I'd known he was a degenerate, but fuck me, he wasn't supposed to enjoy this. How was I going to use torture to make him spill if he enjoyed it?

'You can torture me until I'm dead all you like,' Alfie whispered, his throat hoarse. 'I've got nothing to live for anyway. Who gives a fuck?'

Pathetic.

'Put him away,' I said to Petros, who stood by with his usual unreadable expression. 'And make sure he can't touch that dick.'

I left them there and made my way back to my rooms. My body thrummed with anger. Anger, and an idea.

From following Alfie, I knew that sex was an addiction of his. But what if I could use it against him? Use it to torture him. I had a feeling that his cock drove his stupid little brain more than anything else did.

And I knew damn well that someone could use degradation and humiliation to hurt you. How they could use your own body against you.

At least with Alfie, it was for the greater good. It would save countless others from suffering my fate. For all of those who never made it out.

Pushing down the tiny threads of guilt inside me, I reminded myself that they'd turned me into the monster I'd become. That there was no going back.

Pity wasn't an option.

SEVEN

ALFIE

Discomfort racked my entire body as I lay on the bare mattress, my hands cuffed around one of the bars. All night, people had gawped at me while enjoying drinks and food. While I lay there, my stomach was rumbling with a ferocity I'd never felt before.

My throat rasped as I cleared it, the flesh tender where my blonde tormentor had dug her foot into me. I needed water. And to relieve myself.

Hours passed after the room had emptied, muffled sounds occasionally reaching me from beyond the cavernous room. Water dripped incessantly by the far wall of my caged area, making my bladder ache.

It was bad enough that I'd been stripped completely naked for the woman's amusement, pissing myself wouldn't help my self-esteem any.

Attempting to roll onto my side only made my arms throb more. I tried to stretch them to relieve the pain from where they were fixed to the bars.

Logan's party would have long passed. Would anyone be looking for me? Had even they noticed my absence?

A noise at the far end of the room drew my attention. The hulking, quiet man came into view holding two buckets, one clearly heavier than the other.

My stomach tensed as he opened the cage door, placing the buckets in the middle of the floor. He didn't even glance at me before heading back out and locking the barred door behind him.

Rough hands grabbed at my wrists as he fitted the keys into my cuffs, relief flooding my arms upon being freed.

'Thanks, man,' I said, pulling myself to sitting and rolling my shoulders.

His face was impassive at the other side of the bars. I considered trying to grab him through the bars, pulling him forward and slamming his face into the metal. If I could get the keys...

No.

It was idiotic to think it would do anything other than make him angry. I didn't need someone else to want to tear me to shreds. Not to mention, the outline in his pocket either meant he was exceedingly happy to see me, or he was armed.

'You've got ten minutes. Relieve yourself and get cleaned up.'

'Petros,' I said. He narrowed his eyes, and I continued, 'That's what she called you, didn't she? Tell me, what is the point in cleaning myself if your unhinged lady friend wants to slice me up like an overpriced ham?'

'Because if you don't, you'll go hungry.'

'Would starving myself be worse than whatever fate is intended for me?' I stood as I spoke, my legs wobbling beneath me.

'I'd rather die with a full stomach than without one.' He moved over to the sofa and lay back on it, facing the ceiling.

'Wise words.'

'Get on with it.'

With a sigh, I moved to the empty bucket before glancing back up at the man only a few metres away. 'I'm guessing privacy is out of the question.'

'If you want to wait until you're alone, you're going to end up pissing all over yourself.'

Thank goodness that shame wasn't particularly in my remit of emotions. After I'd finished, I tipped some water on my hands to clean them before plunging my hands into the cold water, taking some to my lips and gulping it down. It hit hard in my empty stomach, only rousing the growling to new heights.

The icy water chilled me to the bone. I worked it over my skin, scrubbing until I felt clean. Petros lay ignoring me the entire time.

What was his deal? Some sort of bodyguard for the crazy blonde? From the way he stared at her like a kid stared at an ice-cream truck, I figured they weren't fucking. While he'd listened to her instructions to take me out in front of the crowd, his body had been tense. After she'd paid me attention, his demeanour rippled with jealousy. Yet there he was, still dealing with me despite his obvious reluctance. Why?

'I'm done,' I said, taking a seat on the edge of the bed and waiting. Petros got to his feet and came over to me, crouching by the bars.

'Left hand.'

I offered it to him and winced as the cuffs bit back into my wrist, attaching one hand to the bars. He came in and removed the buckets before handing me a prepackaged sandwich, crisps and a bottle of water.

The sandwich was terrible; the bread like cardboard and a meagre line of egg near the edge that was displayed in the box. I still ate every crumb. Who knew how long it would be before I got something more substantial?

'Who is she?' I asked, before drinking down a few sips of the water.

Nothing.

'What is this place?'

Nothing.

Sighing, I rubbed a hand over my eyes. I had no concept of what time it was. There were no windows to give an indication either.

'You're in love with her, aren't you?'

That brought Petros' gaze my way. Still no words though. Like talking to a fucking rock.

'How long? I'm guessing for a while. I see it in your face every time you look at her. Does she know?'

Petros cleared his throat before sitting back on the sofa and glancing towards the door. 'You don't know what you're talking about.'

'I do. I've seen it time and again. People falling in love. I've never experienced it myself, but I can see the longing from a mile away.'

'If you've never felt it, how would you know?'

'I've fallen in love with hundreds of people, but only ever for a night. If you don't let it go further, you can't get hurt, right?'

He shrugged, remaining non-committal.

'It makes you seethe when she gives her attention to me, even though it's because she wants to hurt me. You long for even an ounce of that intensity turned towards you. Would you take her boot on your throat to make her happy?'

'You don't know anything about us.'

'I know she's not fucking you. Why? You're hot. She certainly seems like she could do with a good fuck.'

Petros slammed his hand down onto the couch before storming towards me. Fear welled in my chest, but I tried to hide it. I didn't flinch when he thrust his arm through the bars and grasped me by the throat.

'If you talk about her like that again, I'll snap your pathetic fucking neck.'

'You can't,' I said in a choked voice. 'She needs me. And she's holding you at arm's length. Does she need me more than she wants you here?'

His nostrils flared as his fingers tightened their grip.

'I can't wait to see you die,' he snarled.

Intensity bubbled between us as he held me there. God, he really was a good-looking man. It had been a long while since I'd been dominated by a man, and my dick reacted accordingly.

He looked down before letting go of my throat in disgust.

'You sick little fuck, what's wrong with you?' he asked.

'Your blonde isn't the only messed up one around here. If you help me out of here, I could suck the tension right out of you.' It's all I had available to offer.

'I don't want to fuck you.' He reached in and grabbed my other hand, attaching it to the other handcuff so both my wrists were once again attached to the bars.

'You never know, if celibacy isn't making her want you, maybe seeing you with someone else might kick her into action.'

His jaw ticked. He looked like he was seriously considering punching me square in the face.

Instead, he left me there.

'Well, that went well,' I sighed to myself as the door shut behind him.

EIGHT

PETROS

'No fucking way,' I said, my nails digging into my palm.

'It's his weakness, don't you see? We followed him for weeks and what did we see? Him falling between another pair of legs every five minutes. The humiliation did nothing. I can't torture him properly yet because I need him coherent and infection-free. It's perfect.'

'How could you face doing it? After what *he* did?'

Harriet stood facing me, her back to the countertop. 'Because nothing is going to stop me. I don't care if this is the last thing I do, I'm going to kill them all.'

Her eyes glittered, and I swallowed hard. 'You don't need to do it.'

'You don't get to tell me what I need. My whole life I've been told what I need, or what I deserve. I worked fucking hard for my freedom, Petros, and I won't let any man tell me what I can or cannot do. You're either with me or against me.'

My words were like a gobstopper lodged in my throat. I wanted to tell her no. To forbid her from her insane plan of using sex to torture Alfie. She was convinced it would break him. I was convinced it would break me.

Harriet softened at whatever she saw in my face.

'I need someone to play the game with me. Someone I trust who can help me taunt him. Who better than you? You've always been there for me.'

A flicker of hope struck alight.

I dared not breathe in case I huffed it out.

'I know it's not okay to expect you to put yourself in a position to be used to torment him, and I can find someone else if you prefer. It's just that I trust you. You'd never hurt me.'

My brain whirred, trying to put what she was saying into logic. She wanted to use me to to frustrate him? To fuck me?

Having her to myself was all I wanted, but she kept herself closed off from that sort of intimacy. Could I let her use me and go back to nothing afterwards? It would tear me apart. I blinked before looking at her. I wanted to storm over and wrap her in my arms, to tell her to forget it all and to run away with me.

But I couldn't.

Even after the years by her side, she wasn't ready for that.

So, I'd bide my time.

And if that meant accepting whatever scraps she offered, then so be it.

'Okay,' I said. 'I'll help.'

Harriet's smile set my pulse rocketing. Fuck, I'd do anything to see it.

'Thank you. We need to make him desperate. So desperate that he'll be ready to sell the fuckers he's protecting out for a mere whiff of sex. Do you think you'll be able to fake that kind of passion?'

'Oh, I'm sure I'll manage.'

Because what if the old adage 'fake it until you make it' worked? What if I fucked her so damn well that I made her forget that Alfie was even there?

Maybe it was my one chance to make her fall for me.

NINE

HARRIET

I'd left Alfie to stew for three days, having Petros offer food, water and basic exercise as well as the opportunity to wash. Having been in his shoes, I knew how the basics became something to focus on every day. I needed Alfie sane until he broke and gave me my answers.

He sat in the corner, leaning back against the bars, both wrists cuffed to the metal. Despite his predicament, he continued to look as fucking jovial as ever.

'Morning. Or Afternoon, maybe? Thought you'd forgotten all about me, Princess.' Alfie had the audacity to smirk.

A ripple of anger prickled at the endearment. How fucking dare he?

'If you call me that again, you'll lose at least one testicle.'

His knees inched a little tighter together, but he didn't let my threat affect him otherwise. 'You've still not told me your name, which is rather rude given that you are keeping me penned up in your basement.'

Stalking closer to him, I knelt by the bars, reaching through and grasping him firmly by the hair. 'Oh, you'll know who I am. I'm surprised someone with such a smart fucking mouth doesn't have the brains to back it up. You've had days to rack that pathetic little mind of yours.'

The small moan that escaped his mouth surprised me. I dropped my hand as my mouth turned down in disgust.

'My name is Harriet, but I'm more commonly known as The Viper in your circles. Or so I'm led to believe.' I hadn't frequented his circles for quite some time, after all.

Alfie's eyebrows twitched, his mind clearly rifling through to put the name to the rumours he'd likely heard.

'I don't believe in folklore. Tales of a former whore wreaking revenge, a scarred monster disembowelling men. Ridiculous. It's like telling me you're the bloody bogeyman.' His words may have been packed with bluster, but they lacked his usual cocky confidence.

Leaning in close, I gave him a smile. 'Tell me what they say, Alfie? What are the rumours you've heard?'

His hands clenched in his cuffs. 'Nothing. You're just fucking with me.'

Standing, I reached behind me and unzipped my dress, while he watched me like a hawk. 'They told you I was scarred? How about the tattoos?'

'Snakes,' he whispered.

'What they probably didn't mention was the reason for the tattoos. For years, I suffered under the hands of men. Knives. Whips. Cigarettes. Even a brand from one particularly nasty piece of work. I turned and displayed my back to him, his intake of breath telling me the view did the trick. I'd seen my back. I knew. Even with the dark ink etched over the scars, my back was still a mess of knotted, raised, ugly flesh. 'I may well be a scarred monster, but I am a monster of their creation. Like any good horror story, their creation comes back to haunt them.'

'Then why me? I didn't do that to you. I would never...'

Returning my zip to its closed state, I turned back to face him. 'You started it all, Alfie. You were the catalyst that led me here. Without you, I would have had a life. Instead, I'm going to bring death to them all.'

Alfie's face warred with expression. Pity. Confusion. Anger. He still didn't know me. Why would he remember? I was just another hole to him.

'Let's see if I can jog your memory, shall I?'

I took the key from Petros and entered the caged area, coming to a stop in front of Alfie before crouching to his eye level. 'Take a good look at my face. It's been a long time since you last saw it. Over twenty years. You may remember it being softer, sweeter, or maybe pained and streaked with tears.'

Nothing. Not a glimmer of recognition. Anger flared inside me that such a pivotal moment in my life meant nothing to him. Tossing the keys aside, I reached into my pocket and pulled out a flick knife. Alfie's eyes bugged as I bared the blade and twirled it in my fingers.

'It was your eighteenth birthday. And two days after mine. My friend and I had taken the train up to Glasgow to celebrate. A whole weekend of fun. When a woman approached us and asked if we wanted to help celebrate a party, we turned her down.'

I leant forward as I spoke and prickled the end of my knife against Alfie's chest. The muscles in his arms tensed, the cuffs clanking against the metal, but there was little he could do bar trying to kick me away. He seemed wise enough to figure that that might not be in his best interest.

'I didn't think much of it when we saw her in a bar later that evening. She even bought us each a drink. That was the last time I saw my friend. I woke up, groggy in a castle, and I was told in no uncertain terms that if I wanted to live, I had to pretend to want to be there. They chose me—especially for you—based on what you wanted. They just took me.'

There it was. A flicker of recognition in his eyes. Just a hint.

'I was out of it. I didn't want to be there. My father had forced me to go. I'd taken a whole bunch of pills from the medicine cabinet and downed them with half a bottle of Jack Daniels. It's all a jumble.' Alfie's words spilled out like a stream of fogged consciousness.

'You took my virginity while I cried into the couch, with everybody watching and cheering you on. You didn't even speak to me. Just used me. And then forgot.'

Bloody droplets ballooned on his chest as I scored the tip of the knife over his skin. The way his face contorted as he inhaled through his teeth made me smile, I poured my pain into marking him, and I felt a little lighter for the first time in years.

TEN

ALFIE

Pain seared against my chest as she drew the sharp blade over me.

I tried to recall that night. The alcohol and pills had made it seem almost like a fever dream. I'd never have fucked her against her will. I didn't even want to have sex, back then. My father had made me.

'My dad told me that you were an escort. That you wanted it. He told me I had no choice. He was sick of me being a disappointment to him, and that I could at least man up in one respect. I'm sorry, Harriet. I had no idea.'

Blonde waves fell in front of her face as her eyes glistened. She pressed the knife against her throat, and everything around me dimmed to the feeling of the metal against my pulse.

'Truly, I'm so sorry. I know it doesn't make it better, I can't undo what I did. I'm sorry that I didn't even know I'd hurt you—'

'Shut up,' she seethed. 'Your words mean nothing to me. Lies from a degenerate. I don't believe a fucking thing that comes from your mouth.'

'It's true,' I whispered, holding her gaze while the knife pressed harder.

'Even if it was, you left me there, for them. I barely made it through the night. By morning, they had decided that I couldn't go home after what they had done, and they gave me to the man who bid the most.'

My stomach twisted at her words, guilt washing through me.

'I'm sorry,' I said again, at a loss for words.

'You will be.'

The pressure left my throat, and she left without another word.

Petros didn't even offer me a glance as he fetched the keys and locked me back in, blood slowly dripping from the large score mark on my chest. Her words echoed through my head, bringing pain with every one. I'd prided myself on always being an excellent lover, on prioritising others' pleasure and making people's fantasies come true. Could I really have taken her without her consent like that? Trying to force my mind back to that night was met with fog. Snippets of anger and shame. My father had been so disappointed with the introverted son he'd acquired, he'd wanted someone just like him. I was too effeminate. Too shy. A letdown. He'd told me that I'd be attending my party whether I liked it or not and that I'd become a man that night, whether I liked it or not.

And I had.

The praise he'd showered me with at finally sinking into his hedonistic world was the first I'd ever received, and I fell down the path of seeking his approval, one sordid act at a time.

But at what cost?

No food came for hours. No water. Nothing.

By the time people began filtering in, I was parched, hungry and needing to use the facilities. Women watched me with interest as I sat dejected, having been left with nothing but my cruel thoughts to plague me. The reality of what I did to Harriet ate away at me. I may have been out of my mind at the time and unaware of the wounds my actions had caused, but with the passing hours and scouring my fragmented memories, I knew she spoke the truth. Perhaps I deserved to be locked up like an animal.

A group of women came close to the cage, whispering to one another while watching me. A brunette held a plate of hors d'oeuvres that made my mouth water. The tiny crackers loaded with a myriad of toppings made my stomach growl loudly as I struggled to tear my eyes from the morsels.

'Did you hear that?' she said, her laughter making my cheeks burn.

'I don't know what he did, but he must have really pissed Harriet off for her to be keeping him like a dog. Usually, she just kills them.' The woman in the middle of the trio spoke like I wasn't perfectly able to understand what she said. Exhaustion and discomfort attacked me while I listened to their chatter. The younger woman on the end watched me intently, her eyes flicking from the scabbed-over cut on my chest to my pierced dick. I'd given up hiding it. I'd never been particularly modest, but it was far from the least of my worries. The room beyond my bars was filling up quickly, busier than I'd seen it in my time there. At least, I thought it was days. Without any daylight, it was hard to keep track.

'Why's it so busy,' I asked the younger woman, my throat cracking.

She ignored me completely. So much for a potential soft touch. The doors opened, and Harriet appeared, looking devastating in a tight red dress and black biker boots. All eyes turned to her as a hush fell over the gathering. The young woman took the plate of food from her friend while they went off to find somewhere to sit. She faced away from me, and I closed my eyes at the nearness of the food and my complete inability to seize it with my confined arms. The savoury, salty smell of the cheese and meats filled my nostrils. It was torturous.

'Quick,' a heated whisper said.

Opening my eyes revealed her fingertips held behind her back, the loaded cracker only centimetres from my lips. I didn't hesitate to lean forward and catch it between my teeth. Flavour exploded against my tongue, and I could have sobbed with relief had I not had another cracker briskly shoved against my lips.

'Thank you,' I mumbled.

Harriet was busy instructing another man to lower a chain from the ceiling in the centre of the room. Sweat pricked at the back of my neck and she fitted two shackles to the bottom, testing them with a sharp tug.

Fuck, what was she going to do to me?

Another cracker appeared, and while I ate it, the taste had turned to ash in my mouth as fear gripped me.

An excited babble rumbled throughout the crowd. Clearly, they knew what this meant.

'What will she do?' I whispered to the woman who still faced away from me, pretending not to finger-feed me.

There was a hesitation before she shook her head. 'I can't say.'

'You can't or you don't want to?'

'I'm risking enough to feed you. Take the crackers or don't. You can't eat and chat.'

I'd spoken with my mouth full plenty of times before, and none of the women or men had ever complained.

When she'd pushed the final cracker towards me, she walked off without a backward glance. They were undoubtedly pity crackers, but why? Was it some sort of last fucking meal?

With a grunt, I pulled at my cuffs until they bit into my skin, marking deep red lines into my wrists. Knowing it was fruitless didn't make it any easier to sit there and await Harriet's insanity.

A hiss broke out from near where the doors were, but with the room so packed, I couldn't see why. Craning my neck, I eventually saw Petros leading an overweight man with ruddy cheeks and a dirtied suit through the crowd. A woman, who must have barely been twenty, followed behind them, Harriet's friend, who I'd seen when she pinned me beside the couch, held the woman's hand tightly. The crowd was feral. Women spat at the man as he passed by; others lashed out, catching him with fists or nails. He cursed and tried to fight back, blustering at the treatment. I remained as still as possible, not wanting to attract any of their ire my way.

When he reached Harriet, he aggressively lunged towards her. Petros yanked at the short chain affixed around his neck, stopping him short, his face reddening even further.

'I'll kill you and every cunt in this place. Do you know who I am?'

Harriet gave him a saccharine smile and nodded. 'Westley James Senior. Trusted board member of Stanley-Cooper Bank. Father of three. Husband. Abuser of women. That about sum it up?'

The man glared at her, fury etched into his every wrinkle. 'She's a fucking liar. You're going to believe a stupid little bitch over me? If you're so convinced, report me to the police. Everyone in the UK has a right to a fair trial.'

With a tip of her head, Harriet surveyed her prey. 'A fair trial would be fantastic. It's just a shame that you have so many friends in high places, isn't it? You've had a trial before, last time someone found a woman being kept against her will underneath your home. Yet, she was called crazy. Told she made it all up. Except that we know she didn't, did she, Westley? You just paid your chums to keep their no-good mouths shut and dampen it all down.'

'She was a willing participant in a sex game. There's nothing wrong with a bit of fetish.'

'And what about Eve here? Was she a willing participant too? Because she very much says otherwise.' Harriet glanced at the woman, who looked at her feet.

'She's a lying shit. I fostered her. Spent money sending her to the best schools along with my own daughters, and she's repaying me with her bullshit.'

At that moment, I saw myself in Eve. I too had been taken in by a wealthy man. My father's attention had been every bit transactional, but how much worse was it for her? My father had pushed me into a lifestyle that I hadn't wanted. He'd beat me and torn away any self-esteem I had possessed. But he'd never taken advantage of me in the way I very much expected Westley had with Eve. Despite my predicament, I began to hope Harriet gave him her worst.

'Shame you're an idiot. Did you think that we wouldn't see the videos on your phone? She's not even the only one, is she?' Petros held the man tightly by the neck while Harriet bent down and locked the heavy metal shackles about his ankles.

'Get the fuck off me!' Westley screamed, lashing out without much effect. The chain began to move with a lurching creak, dragging the links back around a spool near the ceiling. Westley fell to his hands and knees with a crunch and a cry as his body was slowly upended. His feet ascended first, smushing his angry red face into the floor. The scrape of his skin against the stone made me want to toss up the crackers I'd just eaten. The mechanism groaned as he was lifted fully off the ground. His high pitched scream echoed throughout the room, so loud that it made me wince. Only a foot or so separated his head from the cold stone flooring below.

Suddenly, my own predicament didn't seem quite so bad.

His face turned a deep crimson as he bobbed like a bloated worm while Harriet paced in front of him.

'Admit to your treatment of Eve, and I might hand you over to the police.'

Westley coughed, sending him jerking on the end of the chain. 'I don't believe you.'

Harriet held out a hand, and Petros reached into his jacket, pulling out the knife she'd cut me with, and placed it in her upturned palm. With his eyes widening, Westley tried to swing at her, his arms flailing in the gap between them. Eve shrunk away, stepping partially behind Petros in a way that made my mouth sour. Terror filled her face at Westley's fury.

'The thing is, I can't let you go, confession or not. You were supposed to be a safe haven for a teen, a place that could finally be home—'

Westley interrupted with a barrage of curses before angrily saying, 'I gave her everything. A home. A family. The best schooling. She's an ungrateful bitch.'

'You didn't give her what she needed. Safety and trust. A place where she could feel like she belonged.' Harriet stepped in close and used her blade to cut the buttons from Westley's shirt, his pale skin exposed from belt to neck. His hands tore at her legs, pummelling her and trying to knock her off balance, but she held firm. Without a flinch, she sank the knife into the area just above his groin as he let out an almighty howl. 'And I'm never going to let you do that to another person.'

The tight muscles in her arm bulged as she dragged the knife downwards, cleaving a great cleft in Westley's stomach. His yowls of pain sent shivers through me as I watched the crowd. Harriet with a look of determination on her face, her arm awash with bright red as blood sprayed outward like a grotesque fountain, the coppery tang filling the air. Petros stood by without any expression on his face. Either he had a kick-ass poker face or he'd watched Harriet gut a man often enough to not be fazed in the slightest. Harriet's friend had turned to hold Eve in her arms, trying to hide the gore from her, but Eve watched with wet eyes as the knife tore his flesh asunder.

Fat, blood and guts tumbled from the hole Harriet had created while Westley spasmed on the chain, shock silencing his screams to a gargled moan. Harriet bent at the knees, staring into his face as his intestines dangled between them in long, bloody ropes.

The crowd either stared aghast or turned their eyes away as Harriet scooped up a handful without so much as a grimace. 'How many times did you choke her, Westley? How many times did you force yourself into her as she begged you to stop? The last fucking thing you're going to taste is your own pathetic guts.'

Reaching forward, she pinched his nose with one hand until he feebly opened his mouth, the blood loss clearly affecting him. She wasted no time in stuffing the pulsing organ into his mouth piece by piece as he heaved and shuddered.

He barely lasted for a minute of barely there struggling, before he succumbed to either the lack of air or the blood loss. His body slackened and stilled.

For long seconds, not a noise filled the room before Harriet turned and met my eyes. The threat was as plain as day.

The Viper was real.

And deadly.

ELEVEN

HARRIET

Blood dripped slowly against the floor, the rhythm almost soothing as I sat on the sofa, patiently waiting for the room to empty of everyone but Nancy, Eve, Petros and me.

A clink from the rear of the room brought another to my attention.

Alfie.

In the heat of brutality, I'd momentarily forgotten all about him. His eyes were ringed with dark circles as he met my stare. Had witnessing Westley's demise been enough to make him relent in his claims of knowing nothing about his father's ring of abusers?

I remained focused on him until he dropped his gaze. Crimson stained one of my arms to the elbow; my knife equally as decorated with blood. I should have felt something, but internally I was numb. The first man I'd ever killed had brought about my freedom, and it had devastated me despite knowing how much he'd deserved it. If Petros hadn't been there to help me through the aftermath, I'd have likely thrown myself off something out of the guilt that gnawed at me. Eventually, the guilt ebbed away and left nothing. A gaping hole where my soul had once resided.

'Sit.' I indicated to the others. Nancy and Eve took chairs facing me, while Petros remained by my side. Eve's eyes were ringed pink, and her hands trembled in her lap.

'He deserved it,' I said. 'You didn't bring that about, he did. You aren't the first woman he hurt, but you are the last. Remind yourself of that when the demons try to pull you under.'

Eve nodded, keeping her head directed away from the eviscerated man.

'We'll make sure you have a solid alibi, and his remains won't be found. Do you want to go back to the family?'

'Only long enough to let it all blow over.' Her voice was soft but confident.

'You'll need to lie to everyone. You'll likely all be questioned. Do you think you'll manage it?'

Her nod affirmed that she did.

'You can never talk about me or this place. It's the only way we can help others. We have a good reach and means to be able to help you. When you're ready, get in touch with Nancy, and we can help you with whatever you need; A place to live, money, university admission, even a job. There are a fuckload of monsters in the world, but even more people who want to help those hurt by them. You might feel alone, but you aren't.'

'Thank you,' she said, finally looking directly at me with a gentle smile.

'And if all else fails, you're welcome here with us. It's not five star accommodation, living beneath the city, but it's safe.'

Nancy took Eve out of the room while Petros and one of the few other men who assisted us released the chain, sending the corpse crashing onto the floor with a wet slop. They gathered it up and worked together to remove it from the room, leaving me to my thoughts. Blood puddled between the stone flooring, seeping into the cracks. It would be a bugger to clean.

The numbness inside me was threatening to overwhelm me, trying to drag me back into the blackness that lurked beneath my skin. Glancing over at Alfie, I figured that he could be a perfect distraction.

I needed to feel something. He was going to die anyway, so why not make him useful in the meantime?

Moving to a keypad-locked safe behind the bar area, I punched in the code and withdrew my gun. The metal was bitterly cold from sitting within the recessed safe, which was set in the stone walls. Its weight felt reassuring in my fingers, and I worked slowly to load it. I didn't intend to kill Alfie yet, but neither would I approach him without the means to if necessary.

My footsteps echoed through the room as I approached the cage, picking up a set of keys en route. The way his throat bobbed as I crouched in front of him made me smile.

'Did you enjoy the show?' I asked, holding the gun lightly in my blood-coated hand.

'A touch gladiatorial, don't you think?' His throat rasped, his lips looking dry.

'Nothing wrong with eradicating pests.'

'Is that what men are to you?'

'Only the dickheads.'

'Like me?' Alfie asked.

'Indeed. Are you thirsty?'

'Yes.'

'Good.'

I stood up and stood over him, his back pressing against the bars. His face was at thigh level, his eyes widening.

'You aren't like most of the men I've tortured, Alfie. I'm going to have to get creative with you. What I do know is that you are an absolute slut. You crave sex like most people need air. Usually, you don't struggle to get it, and I'm going to use that against you until you break.'

His lips grazed my thigh, and a wave of revulsion hit me. A flashback from the last time he'd touched me. There had been no softness then, nothing but shame and pain. He'd used me. It was my turn to use him.'

'Does using me make you any better than those men?' Alfie asked, his lips moving against my thigh as he spoke.

'You made me this way. You didn't care when you fucked me in front of a room full of people.'

'I didn't know.' His words came out in a tortured sigh.

I pressed the barrel of the gun against his shoulder. 'Slide down onto the floor.'

It took him a few minutes to be able to do as I'd said with how his hands were cuffed to the bars. When he was on the floor, I slipped my panties off and saw his pupils dilate. It was working. Now, I just had to get through the disgust of letting his disgusting mouth touch me.

It's just a tool, something to make him desperate.

Straddling his face, I aligned myself with his mouth and pressed the barrel of the gun to his forehead. 'Try to hurt me, and I won't hesitate to put a bullet in your skull.'

I felt the gulp he swallowed before I sat fully down on his face. Using the bar for support with my other hand, I kept my eyes on him. His tongue pressed against me, sliding up against my clit as I stifled a moan. Fuck, it felt good. I hadn't really ever had anyone pleasure me like that. The men who used me over my years in captivity were all about their pleasure unless they were trying to humiliate me in some way. Since escaping, I'd rarely indulged in sex unless it was to lure a man. My own hand did the rest.

Arching my hips, I ground myself against his face, letting the sensation of his tongue wash over me. *Holy shit*. He sucked my clit into his mouth and rolled his tongue around it, pleasure coiling throughout my body. Then he moaned. The vibrations of his groan shuddered through me and made my thighs clench.

'You're such a fuck-up,' I said, my voice breathier than I meant it to be. 'Even with a gun to your head, you're fucking enjoying this, you freak.'

His eyes flicked to mine, dark with his blown pupils before he drove his tongue inside me, causing me to let out a low moan. The sensation made me lose my mind. Reaching down, I thrust my unarmed hand into his hair and rocked my hips, crushing my pussy to his face and taking what I needed. Whether he could breathe or not was his problem as I rode his face, tingles building between my thighs. He struggled beneath me as I pinned him to the floor and aggressively ground his face with my cunt, chasing the orgasm that hung just out of reach.

Heat prickled my chest as I panted, and when I looked back down at him with the gun pressing into his face and his eyes wide, I came hard. Tremors ripped through me as I held his gaze, still wildly rocking against his tongue. The orgasm subsided, and I slid back onto his chest as he took a deep breath, his face wet with my pleasure. Even through my hatred, it was a heady sight.

I stood on shaky legs, looking down at his naked body, his cock stood up against his stomach, glittering with metal studs and dripping precum. Shame such an impressive cock was wasted on such a scumbag.

'Please?' he whispered, his dick jerking.

'Please, what?'

'Please let me take care of it.'

I laughed and shook my head. 'This is only the beginning, you sex-mad fuck. By the time I'm through with you, you'll be begging me to sever it to save you the pain of never finishing.'

The door opened at the far end of the room as Petros appeared, cleaning supplies in hand. My cheeks flamed as he took one long look at my rumpled dress, Alfie's wet face and erect dick. I cleared my throat and stepped away from Alfie, walking out of the cage without another look.

'Can you see he's fed and watered after you're finished?' I asked Petros.

He seemed even more tense than usual as his fingers whitening around the mop handle. 'Sure.'

'It's working,' I whispered as I passed him, giving him a wink.

He'd be desperate to give us the information we wanted soon enough.

TWELVE
ALFIE

Fucking hell.

I lay on the floor reeling from Harriet's surprise use of me, and her swift exit afterwards. With my cock still straining painfully, I struggled backwards, huffing until I finally got myself seated upright once more. Couldn't even wipe my damn face. I should have been angry, she'd violated me, but instead, the taste of her still filled my mouth, and her heady scent clung to me.

Between the butchery I'd just witnessed, and having a gun held to my head, I really shouldn't have enjoyed her taking control of me like that.

But I did.

The back-and-forth scrape of a scrubbing brush brought my attention over to Petros, who cleaned at the blood stains with angry strokes. He wore jealousy like a mask; his face pulled into a stoic expression but every part of his body screamed with internalised rage. It was evident in the clenching of his jaw, and the harshness of his strokes. In the way he absolutely didn't look towards me, yet his fury washed from him in waves that crashed against me.

For once, though, I kept my mouth shut.

The clean-up took some time. Bucket after bucket of water sloshed over the stone, rivulets of crimson water running across the other side of my caged area and towards a small drain in the corner. By the time Petros came into the cage and unlocked me from the bars, securing my wrists together, I was tired, hungry and miserable again.

The buckets were back, and I didn't bother to wait for modesty before relieving myself. Petros' eyes never left me as I washed my hands in the bucket of cool water.

'I didn't ask her to do it,' I said, standing and facing him, my eyes darting to the open cage door.

'None of my business.'

'Bullshit. You're fucking furious. How long have you wanted to taste her? And you walked in just after she came in my mouth.' Provoking him was dangerous, but I needed an opportunity to get away or to force him to break down the walls he'd built around himself. Befriend him or cause him to get so angry that he'd make stupid mistakes. And hope he didn't just kick my ass.

'Shut the fuck up and get yourself cleaned up.'

'Why? Is Harriet coming back to suck my dick?'

Within a breath he was on me, his hand around my throat as he pressed me harshly against the bars, pinning me roughly. Pain gripped my throat while he drew his face close to mine. 'If you ever talk about her like that again, I'll skin you alive, you piece of shit.'

Up close, he smelled of a fresh, almost citrus aftershave. Clean and so far from the damp smell of my stone-floored cell. He narrowed his deep brown eyes, hatred filling them.

'Kill me,' I whispered.

'I can't,' he replied through his teeth, his body pressing against mine. The heat from his muscled thighs sent me back into a spiral of lust. Unbidden, my cock thickened against his leg. With his hand still wrapped around my throat, I closed my eyes.

'Taste her,' I said. 'She's still all over my mouth. Take from me what she won't give you.'

His intake of breath was audible, and when I opened my eyes, his face warred with a mixture of disgust and desire. Not for me, I didn't think, but for Harriet. Taking a chance, I put pressure against his hand with my neck until our lips were millimetres apart.

'Can you smell her?'

Petros' eyes closed as he inhaled deeply.

'Fuck,' he groaned.

'Take what you need,' I whispered.

'Why?'

'Why not? How long have you craved her? Lusted for her? Loved her?' His heat encompassed me with our nearness, and my brain fogged from my mission to distract him. Fogged with the familiar drag of my addiction to lust.

Petros' breath swept over my lips as he stared at me intently. His gaze dropped to my mouth as he leaned in a fraction, enough to make me confident he wanted to taste her. Closing the space between us, I captured his mouth with mine, my eyes closing as his body stiffened against my touch. We stayed there, frozen, for a few moments before his mouth opened, his tongue licking over my lower lip.

His moan lit a fire within me. Crushing into his lips further, I kissed him fervently as he lost himself in trying to take every ounce of her from me. Citrus filled my nostrils, mingling with the scent of her, while I grew drunk on every firm stroke of his tongue.

Breaking the devouring of my face, he mumbled against my lips, 'I love her.'

'I know,' I responded, arching my leg between his thighs, finding him just as hard as I.

Clarity seemed to hit him like a freight train as the skim of his dick. Dropping his hand from my throat, he took a few steps back, looking mortified at his actions.

'Petros, let me help. I can help you win her over if you help convince her to let me go.'

Redness seeped into his cheeks, and he ran his hand through his hair, that impassive mask settling back over his face. 'Clean yourself up. All of you. You have five minutes, or you'll go hungry and thirsty again today.'

He didn't look at me for the duration of the time I cleaned myself with the cold water. Nor when he locked me back in and tossed some prepackaged food through the bars along with a bottle of water. I ate in silence, shame wrapping around me at the rejection. It was crazy—he was one of the people holding me captive. But it didn't make it hurt any less. The lack of real human contact was beginning to make me ache.

Despite the hurt, I was still rock solid when he attached my wrists back to the bars. Humiliation washed over me at the fact I couldn't even deal with my own cock. Harriet was right, I was nothing but a sick freak because even that humiliation only made my erection harder.

THIRTEEN

PETROS

The sound of my footsteps echoing through the old stone tunnels clashed with the intense buzzing in my ears. What the fuck had just happened? How had I let him goad me like that? I'd underestimated what a wily fucker Alfie was. Walking in and seeing the glow on Harriet's face after taking her pleasure from him had left me filled with a palpable rage. I'd been tempted to cut his motherfucking tongue out to stop it ever happening again.

But up close. I could smell her on him. It was like her scent possessed me, and the offer of a taste of it, even second-hand, was intoxicating. Taking the taste of her from another man was humiliating, yet I couldn't deny that I'd been as hard as Alfie had. I'd never felt compelled to kiss a man before, but neither could I deny that his kiss possessed a skill that had rendered my brain a foggy mess.

Cold air wrapped around me as I neared our rooms. Could I face her knowing what I'd just done? What she'd done? The idea to use sex to taunt him had been madcap enough when she'd suggested it, but I'd relented thinking it would be us taunting him together. For her to be the one using him alone felt like being split open as brutally as Westley had been. How could I deal with it?

Harriet was sitting on the old, tatty sofa as I entered our main living space, and she jumped up, that glow still filling her cheeks. Jealousy stormed up inside me, and it took everything I had to try and temper it down.

'Oh my God! Did you see Alfie? It worked. He's going to go mad if he can't find relief.'

'Mmm,' I responded, making my way to the fridge and grabbing a beer. It opened with a satisfying hiss as I knocked it on the edge of the counter. The bubbles hit my tongue, and I closed my eyes to avoid looking at her beautiful, excited face.

'We need a plan to ramp it up. Make him so on edge that he'll spill everything he knows.'

'I'm going to shower,' I said, struggling to hide my feelings. I'd thrust them below the surface for years, why now? I just needed some space. To let it blow over.

'Of course. Sorry, I should have thanked you for dealing with the mess. Go, shower. We can conspire together later.'

I forced a smile onto my face with a nod. It wasn't her fault I felt the way I did. She'd made it clear enough over the years that she saw me as a friend, a co-conspirator and fellow vengeance seeker. Our past bonded us, but she didn't have the same depth of feelings as I did for her.

It was fine.

Torturous, but I'd deal with it as I always did.

Shutting my bedroom door behind me, I clicked the lock into place, and without even moving into the space, I opened my pants and fisted my dick. Her pretty face flashed in my head, her scent still lingering within my nose. With a grunt, I imagined her spread over my bed, my mouth bringing her the pleasure she needed. I'd spend all day there, showing her with every stroke of my tongue how much she meant to me. How worthy she was of my desire and love.

I'd seen her used by countless men over the years. Had to stand by while they systematically destroyed the person she was and created the shell of the woman she had become. I'd tried to protect her, but I was expendable; there to be used in a different way. I wanted to have the chance to heal those wounds, the ones I couldn't stop from happening at the time. To pay my penance with her soft sighs.

My cock throbbed between my fingers as I stroked it roughly, chasing the release that would let me wear my mask for another few hours. To temper the beast who wanted to kill anyone who dared to look at Harriet.

But my imaginary world distorted as Alfie's face came into view, his mouth beside mine, vying for her pleasure. Opening my eyes, I shook my head, trying to dislodge that fucker from my mind. But he persisted. Even my own imagination tortured me. The orgasm was so close, and I needed it to function without exploding with fury. In my mind, Alfie smirked at me before sliding down to the floor while I continued to taste my girl. I imagined spreading her wide over my fingers, feeling her contract around them at the sensation of my tongue. I imagined a hot, wet mouth covering my dick as I did so.

'Shit, no,' I whispered, not wanting to go there. But the thought was a dirty, sordid little nugget that I couldn't shake. I could fuck his throat raw with all the anger I'd never be able to give to Harriet. I could bring her sweet pleasure while hurting him for daring to enjoy her. The muscles in my forearm tensed as I thrust my fist down over my cock, my breath coming in rapid pants. I gave in to the filthy thoughts, letting myself imagine how satisfying it would be to slide my dick deep down his throat while Harriet came screaming my name. Tasting her juices as I deposited my own without a care.

Sweat pricked along my spine, my other hand scraping against the door behind me. Hips jerking, I came hard, white ropes of cum spurting out and blanketing the floor at my feet.

With the conclusion came clarity. Disgust at letting my dirty thoughts include the fucker who had hurt Harriet. Cum dripped from my fingers as I leaned my head back against the door and caught my breath.

Outside my room, I could hear Harriet singing to herself in the kitchen area, another reminder of being so close to her, but her never seeing me in the same way I saw her.

Looking down at the mess, I sighed.

The relief sent calm through my veins, compressing the heat that had filled them upon seeing Alfie's face wet with her orgasm.

I'd be able to exist in her orbit for another day.

FOURTEEN

HARRIET

Alfie lay on his mattress watching me. His gaze boring into me made me itch to look at him, but I curled up on the couch and doom-scrolled on my phone instead. Focusing on the anonymous forums where people vented or celebrated their lives was one of my few pointless hobbies. Mostly pointless, anyway. Sometimes, I saw people in dire domestic situations, and on occasion would see to it that a tragic accident befell their perpetrators.

Mostly, I looked at videos of animals being silly and people fretting over the most mundane things. I'd never been able to use social media—I'd have had no one to add anyway—due to my underground status.

'Do you know he hated me?' Alfie said. I fought the urge to look at him. 'My dad. He and my mum couldn't have kids, and he so desperately wanted a son. So, they *acquired* me. I don't even know where from. There are no official papers. I just seem to have appeared one day. I found that out when I was eleven.'

Although I continued to ignore him, it would be a lie to say that my interest wasn't piqued.

'Over the years, he grew harsher with me. I was geeky, I liked computers and comics and hated hunting and sports. I hung out with girls rather than boys. I think he worried I was gay. I guess he was only partially wrong. One day, he told me he should have picked better. Mum was already gone by then, and it was just him and me rattling around the castle when he was there. Which wasn't often. My dad's butler and housekeeper, Grieves, basically raised me. Didn't judge me.'

I swallowed as I pictured Alfie as a boy, living a life of rejection. My childhood had been the opposite. Filled with love and support.

'As I progressed through my teens, he wanted me to take over Rosenhall, to become *a real man*. Everything I did became a personal affront to him. That night, he told me I had two choices; become a man in public, so he could be proud of me, or leave. You don't know how many times I wish I'd had the balls to leave. To tell him to fuck off. But it meant losing everything; my home, Grieves, everyone I knew. I chose the coward's choice and buckled.'

Letting my eyes meet his felt like a weakness, but I couldn't help it.

'The night I hurt you, I'd taken a bunch of pills and drank myself silly. I'd barely had more than a single glass of wine before then. It was the only way I could force myself into losing my virginity in front of the crowd. I didn't even consider who I was fucking, I was barely present enough to perform, never mind thinking outside my own head. Afterwards, I blacked out and awoke to Grieves forcing his fingers down my throat to make me puke up what I'd taken. For the first time, my dad told me he was proud of me. That I did good. The praise felt like a feast after being starved my entire life.'

I held my tongue, my stomach lurched as I was thrown back to that night. Into his hands grabbing me while his father sneered at me. Into his lacklustre thrusts that lasted all too long for a virgin. I'd long presumed it was disinterest on his part, like I wasn't even enough to enjoy. He'd been in a haze. I hated to admit it, but his words made sense.

'I stumbled down a road of seeking his approval. A sick, twisted road of sexual depravity, always seeking something more extreme so he'd thump me on the back and tell me I did well. It's fucked-up. I know that. But pleasing people became a drug in its own way. Bringing pleasure made me feel needed, even if only for a night. I crave that validation every day. It chases away the loneliness for a little while.' Alfie cleared his throat.

'I still hate you.'

'I know. I understand that.'

God dammit. Why the fuck was he spilling all this shit at me? I narrowed my eyes at him. Was it a manipulation tactic? Was it even true, or was I just being a gullible idiot?

Petros came into the room, and I turned to face him, shoving down all the tumultuous emotions Alfie had dredged up. Pulling myself up straighter, I let the years of hurt settle back onto my shoulders, feeding into the hatred I felt for Alfie. He might have had a shitty dad, but he'd used me, and it had sent me into a world of pain and humiliation. It had dragged me from my happy life, and it would never have happened if that woman hadn't been searching for someone for Alfie.

'Did you see the news?' Petros asked.

'No, why?'

'Seems your muffins did the trick. His body was found this morning.'

I didn't even try to hide the grin that coated my face. 'I hope he suffered.'

Petros sat down on the sofa beside me and passed his phone to me. The article was sparse, saying that he'd been found dead but nothing more at the moment. A rush of satisfaction filled me. Another fucker who could never hurt anyone again.

Sitting up straighter, I leaned into Petros, my lips practically grazing his ear as I dropped my voice low. 'Follow my lead.'

Standing, I draped my legs over Petros, straddling him on the sofa with Alfie off to my right. My hair fell over my face as I pressed my body against Petros' chest.

'Are you sure?' he said as I ran a hand over his jaw.

'He's unravelling already. A few days of tension, and he'll be ready to spill everything.'

Petros' tongue darted out, wetting his lips as he glanced to the side, a small frown turning his lips. My stomach rolled as shame bit at me. Of course, this would be hard on him, he didn't see me as a normal sexual being. He saw me as damaged. Something that needed protection. What was I thinking?

Right as I made the decision to climb off him, his fingers skated up my spine, pulling me to him. His lips scraped my throat, and I smiled. At least he could play the game well enough.

God, his mouth felt good against my throat. I rocked against him and let out an overly loud moan to taunt Alfie. Petros kissed his way down my neck, his touches almost reverent. I'd have thought he'd have played it a little rougher to torture Alfie more, but I let him get on with it as I acted up a storm in his lap. My skirt hitched up around my thighs, and Petros' fingers traced their way up the exposed flesh. Stealing a glance at Alfie through my hair, he lay perfectly still, his piercings clearly evident on the erection he sported.

Perfect.

Warmth filled me as Petros kissed his way along my jaw, getting far too close to my mouth for comfort. Kissing wasn't on the table. It was one thing to use my body to elicit information, but no real intimacy. Not with a man who knew how broken I was, and who I'd have to face every day.

Pivoting in his lap, I straddled him in reverse, angling my body towards Alfie. Using my hand, I directed Petros' fingers beneath my skirt, pulling my panties off in the process. Tossing them to the floor, I spread myself as his fingers slid against my clit. A tremor quaked through me at the soft touch. It would be a lie if I hadn't thought of this moment before, of Petros taking me in his arms and touching me. In the middle of my time with my last abuser, I'd often gone into my head and imagined it was he who was using me to make it more bearable. In my head, he'd done a thousand unspeakable things to me. I'd had notions of him and me running off together so many times during my captivity, but when it had finally happened, he'd never shown any interest in a physical relationship.

The way his fingers swept over me brought a moan tumbling from my lips, the strokes of his fingers were slow and tender. I needed more. Despite the pain I'd suffered in the past, I still craved it. Craved someone being rough with me. Craved the pain and humiliation. Petros wasn't that man. He needed a partner who wasn't fucked in the head. Who didn't dream about being pinned and choked when she slid her fingers beneath the covers at night. Someone who was sweet and lovely. Who didn't gut men for a living.

Glancing up, I met Alfie's eyes. They burned into me. The head of his cock was practically purple as he worked it against the air in desperation. It made my insides quiver. Petros pushed two fingers inside me, audibly squelching with how wet I'd become. Being watched felt forbidden. Dirty. Having a man caged and forced to watch me seek my pleasure with another, and be so physically hard because of his torment, had my thighs trembling.

Rocking my hips, I felt Petros growing hard against me which only made me chase the high faster. I panted, the intensity growing between my thighs. Reaching down, I pressed Petros' palm against my clit, grinding myself against him while keeping my eyes on Alfie.

'Please?' He mouthed at me, the muscles in his tattooed arms straining against the metal cuffs that held him.

His desperation tipped me over the edge as I clamped down onto Petros' fingers while his other arm wrapped about my waist.

'Holy shit,' I moaned as he pistoned his fingers inside me, my cheeks heating as Alfie groaned across the room from us. He'd tipped his body and was grinding the tip of his cock against the metal bars. It was a pathetic sight. So why did it make me come even harder?

My pulse beat erratically as I climbed off Petros' lap and turned, giving him a grin. 'That was perfect, thank you. Look at him!'

Petros' eyebrows creased before he looked past me to where Alfie lay. It seemed he'd almost forgotten he was there.

'Can you make sure he's chained so that he can't get any relief? I need to go get cleaned up.'

Righting my skirt, an awkwardness passed between us. I shoved it deep down.

It was necessary.

FIFTEEN

PETROS

Harriet left me sitting on the couch, nursing a monster erection and glaring at Alfie.

The pathetic fuck was laying there, his cock about bursting from watching Harriet's orgasm. The one I'd finally given her after all the years of dreaming about it. I clenched my fists, anger rising at the fact I'd had to share her pleasure with him.

Grabbing the keys, I unlocked the cage, the barred door slamming back with an incredible clang.

'Just give me five minutes without the chains. Come on, man-to-man, you know what it's like,' Alfie pleaded.

I didn't respond. Grabbing the leg shackles on the chains, I secured them around his ankles, wincing at the intake of his breath when I touched his skin.

'Please?' he begged. His dick protruded from his stomach like a steel-laden ladder, the tip glistening with precum. Fucking hell, I could see why women fawned over him.

Using a crank in the wall opposite, I tightened the chains until Alfie was stretched out over the floor, his upper body on the mattress, where his hands remained attached to the bars. His dark hair was dishevelled on his forehead, his inked skin standing out in the bare cell.

The fantasy of sinking my cock into his mouth crept into my mind like a dark little demon. Swallowing hard, I watched him watching me. My dick still stood thickly against my zip, where Harriet had left me full of pent-up desire. His eyes flicked to the bulge in my pants. My feet moved towards him almost without thought. Crouching beside his head, I took the fingers I'd fucked Harriet with and thrust them into his mouth. The wet heat sent a bolt of need through me that roused both lust and anger. His tongue wrapped my fingers while he stared into my eyes. He neither questioned the action nor tried to move away from the violation of his mouth. If anything, his eyes were hooded with desire.

'Do you taste that?' I said through my teeth. 'I did that. She came on my fingers while you lay here like a piece of shit.'

Tilting his head to the side, my fingers slipped from his mouth. With a smirk he said, 'Yeah, but she came looking into my eyes.'

Rage had my hand around his throat. My fingers crushed him tightly. 'Shut the fuck up.'

Alfie's tongue darted out, wetting his lower lip before grazing it with his teeth.

'Make me.'

Fury blew in an eruption from my core and flooded my veins.

I would make him.

Without thinking, I unleashed my cock, pulling it free from my trousers while using my other hand to grip his hair. He put up no resistance as I pushed my dick deep into his mouth, giving him no quarter. His eyelids fluttered as I pressed my hips forward, pushing past the slight narrowing at the back of his throat until I was seated entirely inside of him. The heat that enveloped my cock made my thighs quake. Fuck, it felt good. It had been so damn long.

Shame filled me, but it only served to fuel the fury in my strokes as I fucked his mouth as thoroughly as I would have fucked Harriet's pretty cunt. When his tongue slid against the underside of my shaft, I couldn't help but groan. Alfie's eyes flicked up to mine as he moaned over my length, the vibrations making me weak.

Fuck.

I pumped against his tongue, hitting the back of his throat and making him splutter. I didn't care. I wanted him to hurt for stealing that little bit of joy from me, from sullying her orgasm with his remark. I wanted his throat to burn for the rest of the fucking night. For his balls to ache as he suffered alone in the dark. Thrusting hard, I buried myself to the hilt, grunting. Damn, he felt good around me.

His hands clenched against his cuffs when I picked up speed, fucking his throat hard, pinning him against the mattress with my hips. My orgasm ripped through me with a cry that shocked me. Coming in his mouth was a thousand times better than coming in my fist had been. Tremors shook me as I rode his face, pulling out as the final spurts released, soaking his face in the process.

My chest rose in harsh breaths as I leaned up against the bars and looked down at Alfie's cum-soaked tongue and face. He swallowed it down without the slightest hesitation.

'Help me, please?' he whispered.

Moving back, I took stock of his erection, it looked painfully tight.

'No,' I said, standing and pulling my trousers closed.

Shame made my fingers shake as I closed my zip. I had never been into men, why the fuck had I done that?

He goaded me into it.

He deserved it.

My skin prickled in the aftermath of my orgasm.

'It's okay to enjoy it,' Alfie said.

'Shut up.'

'Are you going to make me again?'

With a growl of exasperation, I left him there, slamming the cage closed and stalking off to my room. The situation couldn't stay as it was. It was going to drive me crazy.

But convincing Harriet to let a plan go never went well.

Her need for revenge outweighed anything else. I didn't doubt that if I got in the way of it, she would cut me off completely.

The only other option was to make him talk sooner rather than later.

Upping the ante.

Crushing his spirit.

When I closed my eyes later that night, all I could see was his cum-coated smirk.

SIXTEEN

ALFIE

In what I could only assume were the days following Petros' use of my mouth, he barely looked at me, far less uttered a word to me. When he came into my cage and unlocked me entirely, while holding a gun, confusion made me hesitate.

'Up,' he barked.

My limbs were stiff and ached terribly as I used the bars to pull myself upright. Deep, red indents gouged into my wrists where I'd been cuffed for so long. Petros' face was utterly impassive as he walked out of the cage before standing and waiting for me.

'Grab the brush and get sweeping the cage. Harriet thinks you need to move more, so get moving.'

I did as he asked, every part of me screaming in protest at the change of position. With the meagre rations of food and water, and the inactivity, my skin looked pale and sunken. The swish of the brush as I scraped it against the floor was the sole sound in the cavernous room. I missed my freedom. I missed clothes. I missed the faces of the few people who I had in my life. Captivity weighed around me like an anchor made from pure melancholy. My shoulders slumped as I swept, dragging me down with my dejected mood. Finding the pep to try and sweet talk my captors was getting harder by the minute.

Eventually, there was a neat pile of dust and debris outside the cage. Petros handed me a scrubbing brush and a pale of warm soapy water. Plunging my hands into the warmth was enough to elicit a moan. I couldn't remember the last time I'd felt warm. I had no clothing, no blankets, and the room was damp and chilly. Bar my bare mattress, it was all icy stone and metal bars.

'Get on with it,' Petros said. I glanced up at him just in time to see him eradicate a brief softness from his face. I must have looked as pathetic as I felt.

Scrubbing the dirty floor took forever. The water was nearly cold and a murky brown by the time I finished. Brown splatters covered my legs and arms, exhaustion sinking into my very bones.

'Come on,' Petros said. He fitted the cuffs back over my wrists, making me wince as they bit back into the already-marked flesh.

Gripping my arm in his wide fingers, he walked me out of the room and through a corridor made of the same rounded stone tunnel as my prison. He opened a door and shoved me into a sparsely furnished room. My eyes settled on a tin bath, the water in it soapy and steaming. I could have cried. A lump formed in my throat.

'Is this a trick?' I asked.

'No, get your ass in before I change my mind.'

I needed no further prompting.

The heat nipped at my legs as I climbed in, but I sank down into the hot water without a thought, welcoming the redness that flushed my body. Holy Mother of God. Scooping up some water, I pressed it to my face, revelling in the feeling of being warm and clean.

Petros sat on a wooden chair, his gun resting on his thigh as he watched me.

'Why?' I asked.

'She wants you clean, for tonight.'

Fear rippled in my stomach. Swiftly followed by a flash of lust. Fuck, did she want to kill me or torment me? 'What's happening tonight?'

'A get-together in the bar. You were stinking it out.'

I sank back against the edge of the small tub, closing my eyes and letting the heat envelop me like a moist hug. A few minutes passed in silence before there was a knock on the door. Petros answered it, keeping an eye on me while taking a paper bag from someone on the other side.

He handed it to me along with a paper cup with a straw poking out.

'Eat,' he said, retaking his position on the wooden chair.

My cuffed hands made putting the cup down on the floor difficult. After placing it beside the bath, I peered into the grease-soaked bag. It contained two burgers and a large portion of fries. They were still hot, and their salty, greasy smell made my mouth water. The idea that she could well have poisoned then flitted through my mind, I'd caught the gist from the discussions about the MP who died. I'd heard enough to know it hadn't been her first dabble with poison. My stomach growled at my hesitation, and I figured that death by burger was better than nothing.

Flavour exploded in my mouth. I'd never been one for regularly eating cheap takeout, only really when I was with friends who wanted to, but it was the most glorious thing I'd ever tasted. I made quick work of the first burger, before devouring the second. My stomach protested when I added the fizzy cola to the mix, the sugar sending waves of delight through me. I'd eaten so little in the previous days that I knew I was in danger of throwing it all up. I still started on the salty fries, their slight sogginess not remotely putting me off.

'Is this a guilt meal?' I said when I was halfway through the food.

'How about just fucking eating it?'

I shrugged and stuffed some more fries into my mouth, groaning at the salt-laden potato-y heaven.

'She needs something I don't think you can give her.' I put the empty wrapper on the floor after hoovering up the last of the fries and sat back in the bath. Petros fought the urge to reply, his fingers clenching the stock of his gun as his mouth opened and then closed.

'What?' he asked, curiosity winning out.

'I've met, and slept with, a lot of people over the past twenty years. Some come to my hedonistic resort to spice up their lives, others to live out fantasies. But some come looking to heal. Some people who go through extreme abuse crave elements of it in a scenario they can control, to deal with it in a way.'

Petros' jaw ticked, and his eyes narrowed. 'She doesn't want to be hurt. I saw her go through that, it tore her apart every fucking day.'

'There's every chance I'm wrong, but I don't think so. You protect her, and you saw her in the worst situations, right?'

A curt nod was all the answer I got.

'She doesn't want you to see her like that again. To know she might need *that*. She probably thinks you'll look down on her. You've worked hard all this time to help her out of the situation.'

He pursed his lips while I spoke, his dark eyes fixed on my face while his fingers gripped his gun in a way that made me want to duck out of the way. But he was listening. This was the closest I'd got to getting someone onside.

'I can't do that to her,' he said, finally.

'I know. But she needs what you are giving her too. She needs to feel loved. To be worshipped. To have that person who knows the softer side that I'm sure she must have somewhere beneath the anger.' The water sloshed around me as I sat up, putting my elbows on the edge of the bath and resting my chin on one hand, the other dangling, still cuffed.

Petros seemed to snap out of the conversation, his face flushing as he suddenly stood.

'Get out. It's time to go.'

The chill hit me as soon as I got up, and I only hoped the tenuous bridge I was trying to form with him would hold.

Because Lord help me, I needed it to.

SEVENTEEN

PETROS

The bar area was beginning to thin out at long last. Being present tonight had proved nigh on impossible as Alfie's words had plagued my head like a pesky group of biting mosquitoes. Stealing a glance at Harriet, for what must have been the millionth time that night, I watched the way she chatted with Nancy and a few of the others. Her body language was relaxed and open in a way that I knew was false. She gave the impression of being easy going and in control, but I'd been there on the nights when she fell apart as soon as we got back to our private rooms. I'd seen her take a baseball bat to a piece of furniture, unable to stop until it was obliterated into a thousand tiny pieces.

It was all an act.

Could she be hiding the fact she craved darker desires? And why couldn't I be comfortable fulfilling them? The thought of closing my fingers around her throat in the way I had done to Alfie gave me a visceral reaction. My stomach heaved at the thought of inflicting any pain on her. I'd been forced to witness the abuse she and others had suffered for years. There wasn't a chance I could emulate it, even if I knew Harriet needed it.

Pain lashed at my chest as I came to a realisation. I'd never be enough for her.

Even if she accepted my adoration, she'd always be wanting more. Needing a man who could reach into her and toy with the darkness within her core

How could I ever deny her what she *needed*?

The room emptied as minutes passed until, eventually, only Harriet and I remained. Well, and Alfie, who sat in his cage.

With her boots clipping on the stone floor, she sidled up to me with a wicked gleam in her eyes.

'It's time,' she whispered.

A wave of panic brimmed in my throat as I stole a look at Alfie.

'What do you have in mind?'

'I want you to fuck me.' I don't know what emotion showed on my face, but she closed her eyes and inhaled sharply. 'I know it's awkward, but you did so well at acting it out before, I need you to help me.'

I wanted to grip her by the chin and spew my feelings out to her. To tell her that there was no acting. That I'd thought about touching her for years. Guilt had eaten away my bravado, but it had never been a lack of interest. Alfie's statements rang through my head as I looked into her pretty face. I couldn't give her what she needed, but *this* I could do.

'I'm yours for the taking.'

Reaching up, she pressed a hand against my chest before standing up on her tiptoes. Warm lips grazed my throat. 'Thank you, follow my lead.'

Anywhere.

She took my hand and walked me to Alfie's caged area, unlocking it and entering.

'Good evening, Alfie. Did you enjoy the party?'

'Oh yea, thrilling,' he responded with his usual level of sass.

'Are you ready to talk yet? To drop the names of your father's associates.'

Alfie turned his head with a sigh, looking up at her quite earnestly. 'I don't know them.'

'So, you're saying you were forced by your father to play the sex games he required, yet you never met the pervs he had in his inner circle?'

'Not that I know of. Rosehall has had so many regulars over the years, but you can't go killing everyone in case they are guilty.'

'I can. And if I have to I will. Give me a name,' Harriet demanded.

'No.' Alfie's face was set in determination.

'So be it.'

Harriet turned towards me and reached up, feeding her hands into my hair and tipping my head backward. Her teeth sunk into my neck, and she dragged a moan from me. I knew it was her rage at Alfie's refusal spurring her actions on, but the moment she touched me, I lost the will to care.

Fuck the why.

For the next short period of time, she was mine. Audience or not.

The material of her dress shifted beneath my fingers as I stroked them up her back, feeling the hard, knotted flesh beneath. The way her tongue bathed the bite mark on my throat sent me into a flurry of lust. Scooping her ass up with my hands, I lifted one of her thighs onto my waist and rocked my hips. My hardening dick grazed against her core, and the way her breath hitched made me feral. I repeated the movement, groaning as her heat reached me through the fabric between us.

God, I wanted to kiss her. Every time I tried, she'd move her mouth to my neck or jaw. It was infuriating. If she wouldn't let me press my tongue against hers, I'd show her what it could do elsewhere. She stood right next to where Alfie lay, and when I dropped to my knees before her, my thigh grazed his head.

Without waiting, I leaned forward and slid her dress up over her hips, fitting my mouth over her panties. The way she trembled at the touch sent me wild. I'd claim her back with my tongue. Taste her for myself while Alfie had to watch.

I pulled one of her thighs over my shoulder, slipping her panties to the side and sinking my tongue deep inside her wet cunt. The gravitas of the moment, after so many fucking years of dreaming about it, wasn't lost on me. Finally, I felt at home.

Her moans echoed in the room as I worked her with my tongue, giving my all. I needed her to come against my face, to taste her pleasure for myself.

'Fuck, his mouth feels so good,' she said. I glanced up to see her watching Alfie.

Jealousy ripped at my nerves. I wanted her to focus on what I was doing. Not on that cocky little fuck. I doubled down on her cunt, sucking her clit into my mouth and rolling it with my tongue. Her hands fitted into my hair, tugging sharply as I gripped her ass in my hands, holding her tightly to my face.

'Holy fuck,' she moaned.

Mine. I thought, possessiveness only urging my tongue on.

Her legs trembled, and I pinned her to my face, moaning into her cunt as she came. Pain filled my scalp when she gripped my hair between her fingers, her hips rocking against me. I swallowed every tremor she gave. It wasn't enough. I needed more of her.

Pulling her downwards, I bent her over Alfie, her knees on either side of his face, her ass high enough that he couldn't use his mouth on her. She was mine. And I'd fucking show them both.

Freeing my dick from my pants, I slid it deep inside her without a second thought. I paused when I was fully seated inside her still-pulsating pussy, my mind blown by the intense heat. This had been too long coming.

There was no holding back.

EIGHTEEN

HARRIET

My mind blurred as Petros shifted behind me, his dick sunk to the balls inside me. He was thick, stretching me around his girth. I don't know what I'd expected when I asked him to help me, but the tumultuous emotions clouding my mind weren't it.

For years, he'd almost been a brother to me. Him being inside me felt wrong. But at the same time, so fucking right. It had been a very long time since I'd willingly let a man inside me, and even then, only for ulterior motives. To make them let down their guard so I could drug them or kill them.

This is a game too, I reminded myself. *He is following your orders.*

The thought brought a stab of humiliation. I focused on Alfie's painfully red erection in front of me. My hands were pressed over his thighs, either side of his dick, for support as Petros pulled back and thrust into me. His strokes were harried and sure, his hips arcing in a way that made my insides weep with need.

I wanted him to reach out and grab my hair or press his fingers to my throat. To tell me I was a worthless little whore. It was fucked-up. But making me feel like my body was betraying me almost excused the pleasure that was inflicted on me. Petros' hands smoothed over my hips, holding my dress over my ass. He probably didn't want to see the network of scars over it. Didn't want to remember what I had been. Probably closed his eyes and thought of someone else to get through it.

Still, the artful way he slid his dick inside me made my body remember. Remember what it felt like to be brought to orgasm at someone else's hands. Coming on a mouth or my own fingers didn't hold the same intensity as being filled, and I couldn't fight back the whimper that fell from my lips.

Petros scooped me up and pulled me to his chest, continuing his deep thrusts as he pinned me to him.

'Fuck,' I moaned.

Alfie's dick bobbed in front of us, his balls looking achingly full. Satisfaction crept into me at the sight. Glancing down, I saw his face below us, his eyes fixed on Petros' dick spreading my cunt around it. A pang of jealousy filled me. I'd have loved to see what we looked like from his point of view. The sordidness of our actions being above him sent a ripple of lust through me. What we were doing was filthy. *Despicable.* Damn, it made me clench over Petros' cock.

Alfie's eyes flicked to mine, and it was like he set a firework inside me. Pleasure ricocheted through me as he held my gaze. Petros' hot breath grazed my neck as he growled, and the animalistic noise only added to my growing pleasure.

One of Petros' hands slipped between my thighs, caressing my clit, and I lost any semblance of resistance. I came so hard that a gush of liquid escaped me and rained down over Alfie, each one of Petros' continued thrusts sending more splashing over his face. The sight was positively filthy, and it drew out my orgasm as Petros refused to let up with his harsh strokes. My body quaked, and I rode out the waves like a rag doll in his arms. After another minute, he exploded inside me, my name tearing from his lips in an almost pained cry. Heat filled me as he pressed me firmly to him; holding me there as he pumped viciously in a moment of pure need like I'd never seen him display before. Closing my eyes, I let the tiny sliver of pure pleasure feel real. Being wrapped in his arms like a lover, filling me with his cum like I wasn't a broken husk of a woman. Like the kind of intimacy other people had.

His lips pressing against my neck broke me from my moment of indulgence and brought me back to the real reason Petros was pretending to want me at all.

Alfie.

Shifting, Petros slid out of me, his fingers holding me a second longer, almost as if he was reluctant to depart from his position deep in my cunt.

I turned around to face Alfie, my pussy inches above his face.

With a smile, I clenched, sending a splatter of white cum downward. It hit his lips, and I waited for him to turn his head or revolt from having another man's cum on his face. Instead, his tongue darted out and licked the sticky white mess up. With blown pupils, Alfie looked at my pussy with ravenous desire. Another squeeze dripped more of our cum onto his mouth, and a mix of anger and interest tore through me. Anger because he was such a dirty little fuck that I had no idea how I was going to break him, and interest because the urge to drop down and make him lick Petros' cum directly from me was a heady thought.

But that's what he wanted. I saw it then, in the way his gaze lingered on the cum gathering along my slit. He feeds off the attention. And suffers when he doesn't get it.

'Look at you, you disgusting pig. There is no low you won't stoop to,' I said in sharp, punctuated words.

'Likewise. You're thinking of pressing that cunt to my face right now, aren't you? Thinking about pressing it down over my pierced cock and letting me go so I'll fuck you the way you crave. Fuck you like I hate you.'

Heat flushed my cheeks, and I glanced up, but Petros was nowhere to be seen. I searched the room, wondering where he'd gone.

'He can't take it. He's so in love with you, but he sees you wanting to be used by someone like me, and it kills him.'

'He's not in love with me.' Anger broke out, and I reached down, pressing my fingers against his throat, wanting to cut off his poisonous words.

Alfie gave a broken laugh, his cum-coated face breaking into a delirious grin. 'He worships the fucking ground you walk on.'

'Shut up,' I said. He had to be mocking me. Did he know how badly I wished a man like Petros, someone good and just, could love me? I rained my fists down on him, catching his jaw, his mouth and his throat. His laughter only let up to groan after a few minutes, when my knuckles were bruised and my breath panting.

'You are a hateful fuck, Alfie. It's no wonder your own father couldn't love you. I may have been fucking abused since the night we met, but at least people wanted me. No one has ever *wanted* you, have they?'

Alfie's eyes dimmed before filling with water. He blinked away from me, and I stood, pulling my dress down as rage filled my veins.

He deserved that, I told myself.

His broken look of detachment didn't leave my mind as I walked away and left him there, locked in his cage; alone.

NINETEEN

ALFIE

My stomach had ceased groaning at some point. It hurt to move, but I forced myself to do what I could to stretch out my limbs as often as I could.

How long had it been?

The bucket I'd been given to relieve myself hadn't been removed, and desperation filled my head.

Is this it? Am I going to die in this fucking cage?

Sleep was my only escape, but even that was full of taunting dreams and the illusion of freedom that broke me every time I awoke.

'Stop ignoring me,' I screamed, my throat burning in protest. A fresh drop of water appeared on one of the bars beside me, and I pressed my tongue against it. Where it came from was a mystery, but the semi-steady droplets were all I had to sustain me. Tears pricked my eyes as silence met me, my echoed cries the only sound I'd heard for what felt like forever.

The next time I woke, three slices of plain white bread awaited, along with a bottle of water. I sobbed at the realisation someone had been there and I had missed them. The lack of interaction was making me question my own sanity. I ate the bread slowly, savouring every dry mouthful. Licking the crumbs from my fingers, I took my time sipping the water. Should I save some in case they left me so long again? Or drink it all in case they took it away?

With my ankles chained, I couldn't sit upright fully, nor reach below my navel; every single movement was a bitter struggle.

It had long become clear that no one was coming to save me. Ewen, Logan, Mac and Cam had either given up the search or perhaps hadn't deemed my disappearance worth it. Harriet's biting words smacked into me, bringing additional pain to the physical aches I felt. *No one has ever wanted you, Alfie.*

They hurt most because they were right.

Anger made me fight my bonds, my strength waning and making my attempts pitiful. The cold stone beneath my legs bit whenever I moved from the small warm patch my lengthy containment created. In fuzzy moments, I'd believe I'd heard someone, or had seen movement, but no one heeded my cries.

The sexual torment and pain had hurt me, but the isolation would kill me. It would drive me from my wits until I lost all grip on reality.

'Please?' I begged the silence, my face damp with tears.

'Help?' I asked the darkness, my nails cracking as I dragged them against the stone floor.

'Don't forget me,' I called to nothing.

TWENTY

PETROS

The anger at the situation I'd found myself in fuelled my treatment of Alfie for the first few days after the incident with Harriet. I'd finally given in and given myself to her, but after she'd been focused on him, not me. She'd used my cum to taunt him, and it burned a hole into my chest that I didn't know how to fix.

I'd left before I could see any more, but the thought that she had likely lowered herself onto his wicked tongue was too much to bear.

You fucking idiot.

I cursed myself for believing it could have been anything else, that fucking her would have made her want me. She'd told me it was all an act, and what... I thought my dick could magically make her see fucking butterflies and rainbows?

The cupboard door buckled beneath my fist as I punched it, the pain bringing a moment of sweet relief from the agony inside my head. Whatever had gone down after I'd left, or maybe had gone down because of us fucking, had left Harriet barely saying a word to me. She'd gone out on whatever fucked-up mission she'd chosen without me. For the first time since we'd killed the fucked who owned her, she'd left me.

All because of Alfie.

If it weren't for him being a twisted little fuck, we would never have crossed that threshold. Being intimate with her had been a fantasy of mine for years, but not like that. Not in a way that would tear us apart rather than bring us together.

My knuckles cracked when I balled my hand up, bruises already forming from my violence towards the door. I threw myself down on my bed and closed my eyes. Alfie's pitiful cries broke through. Reaching over to the display system, I punched my finger against the volume control, silencing him. The video feed had plagued me as I watched him dip lower and lower because, despite my anger, I was beginning to think he wasn't the devil Harriet had painted him to be. I didn't doubt that he'd hurt her and that he deserved to pay for that, but the other stuff with his dad? What if he really didn't know anything about it?

It made me sick every time I thought about it. I wanted to protect Harriet, even after everything. It was my duty to protect her. But torturing Alfie didn't feel like it had done with any of the other men we'd destroyed. We'd always had solid evidence of their deeds prior to hurting them. I couldn't discount the pain Alfie had caused her, but he was also forced into the act from what she'd told me. He'd paid for it.

The rest of it was beginning to feel like cruelty for cruelty's sake.

Harriet was in the kitchen area making a cup of tea when I ventured in.

Tension lay thick in the air between us, making me want to retreat. I leaned against the counter and swallowed. 'How'd it go?'

'Another killer removed from the world.'

'Were you careful?'

Harriet narrowed her eyes as she turned, resting back against the fridge and blowing on her steaming mug. 'Aren't I always?'

'No.'

A twisted smile curved her lips, one that had never been turned my way before. A smile usually reserved for men she wanted to hurt. A shiver snaked up my spine, and I stood straighter.

'Are we going to talk about what happened?' I asked, wanting everything to just go back to the way it had been. Pre-Alfie.

'You fucked me, Petros. You bent me over and filled me with your cum. What's there to discuss? We weren't making love. Did it not satisfy you?' A thousand sirens sounded inside my skull. Her eyes flashed with a promise of danger. 'Or did it make you sad to see me drip it into Alfie's mouth? Because that's the reason we were fucking, wasn't it? To torture him.'

I wanted to grab her and tell her that it was more than that. That I had craved her since the day I first laid my eyes on her. Through all the pain and angst, it had always been for her.

'He's ruining everything,' I said, failing to hide the pain in the words, holding my position as she moved towards me, her hot tea sloshing over her fingers. She didn't even flinch. 'I should just go in there and put him out of his misery.'

'It'd be the last thing you do.' Her words were as sharp as her blade, cutting me with their venom-soaked edges. For the first time, I saw her as Alfie did, saw beyond the glinting amber pools in her eyes to the dark soul that lay curved like her viper namesake. He was right, there was a side of her that I wouldn't be able to feed. No matter how much I worshipped her. She needed something that wasn't me. The realisation filled my veins with burning ice.

I love her.

When I was taken from my family and forced into her owner's service, I believed that working hard and following orders would keep my family safe. It hadn't. He'd taken me to pay their debts and killed them anyway. I'd seen my pain reflected in the beautiful, tortured twenty-five-year-old Harriet when I was just seventeen. I had disobeyed my owner for the first time to clean her wounds and wrap her in my arms. My service had been spent making it my mission to save her one day. The day that we killed the dickhead, I had found my family in her. For years, she'd been the sole focus of my attention. The light that kept me burning.

She had always been enough for me, but I'd failed to see that I wasn't enough for her.

What a monumental fucking idiot.

'I need this,' she said after a few minutes of silence stretching between us. Worst of all, I knew it was true. She needed to track down the men who hurt her and make them pay. I no longer believed that it would end there though. Could I spend the rest of my life following her around like a wounded dog, begging for scraps of her attention?

'I know. After this, I'm done.' Was it pain or anger that shone in her eyes at my words?

'So be it.'

Alfie looked pale and lost as I approached the cage. Guilt ripped at my innards. He may have been our captive, but in our anger, we'd mostly left him without having even his basic needs met. Food, water, soap, company. Even we'd been afforded that.

He didn't move when I opened the cage and the worry that he was dead sank into me. Only when I saw the slow rise of his chest, did I let myself breathe. A soft groan was all that met me as I detached his leg shackles and unclipped his hands from the bars, keeping his wrists cuffed together. Lifting him was too easy. His once-pronounced muscles were looking sinewy and waxy in the low light, and concern flooded me. I shouldn't have cared, but the sassy fuck had grown on me despite my anger at Harriet's attention towards him. With my arms beginning to strain, I made my way to my room, not caring if Harriet saw me.

The kitchen and sitting room area were empty, so I pushed my way into my room and placed Alfie down on my bed. Leaning over him, I pinched his chin between my fingers and spoke into his ear.

'I swear if you cause me any grief, I'll throw you back in that cage and leave you there. Don't try anything stupid.'

'Okay,' he said in a throttled whisper, his throat rasping.

I filled the tin tub in my small bathroom before lifting Alfie into the water. Leaving him there, sitting upright, I fetched some electrolyte salt replacement sachets and a bottle of water, combining them and grabbing some snacks from the cupboard. Prepackaged ones just in case my argument with Harriet had led to any of her deadly cooking.

Alfie's hands trembled, spilling some of the drink into the bath water, so I took the bottle from him and held it to his lips as he drank deeply.

'Not too quickly, you'll throw up. Take it easy.'

'Why?'

I creased my brow. 'I just told you why.'

'No. Why are you helping me?'

I considered my response, making him take a few more small sips as I did.

'Because I believe you. I know you hurt her, but I'm not sure you were given much more choice than she was. More than that, I don't think you know jack shit about what your dad was up to.' The words felt like a betrayal to Harriet, but as I released them, letting them become real, I knew I believed them wholeheartedly.

'Thank you. Will you help me get out?'

With a shake of my head, I declined. 'I can't. She'd kill us both.'

'She'll kill me anyway,' Alfie said dejectedly, his eyes closing as he leaned back in the water.

Moving behind him, I scooped up water in the small jug I kept by the bath, pouring it over Alfie's crusted hair.

'You need to give her something to go on. Some sort of hope.'

'My dad's dead. He couldn't give me the names even if I tried.' Alfie moaned softly as I worked my fingers into his hair before adding some shampoo and lathering it up. A sob racked his shoulders. 'I'm sorry, it's been so long since I felt something kind.'

Swallowing, I didn't speak, just continued to work my bubble-covered fingers against his scalp. It was surprisingly intimate and very soothing. It had been a long time since I'd been touched, or touched someone, with kindness too. Not since the day I was taken.

The sweet, citrusy smell of the shampoo filled my nostrils as I let the moment just exist. I didn't try to question it, not let any of the guilt or pain take me from it. Two souls taking a break from the pain with lathered fingers.

Just as swiftly, I cleared my throat and let the moment fall between my fingers like grains of sand. Some things were there to be clung to, while others you had to hold for a short time before letting them go. Alfie scrubbed at his face and body, the movements seeming to make him flag by the minute. Handing him a towel, I waited for him to dry himself, and fetched him a pair of jogging bottoms. They hung loose around his hips where he was much slighter than I; far more of a lithe, toned figure to my more meaty body.

He sat on my bed, picking through the snacks, trying to eat them with a level of decorum that must have pained him to muster. He was a man quite literally starved. Locking my door, I put the key in my back pocket before joining him on the bed, laying back and resting my head on my pillow. The blank stone above us was the same as it had been in all the years I had spent in our hidden bunker world beneath Glasgow, yet it looked different. I noticed a crack I'd failed to see in all my years staring up at it. Had it changed, or was it my perspective?

Groaning and holding his stomach, Alfie lay next to me. 'I'm going to regret eating all of that.'

'If you puke on my bed, I'll be pissed.'

Alfie turned his body towards me, his cuffed hands sliding up between the pillow and his cheek. 'Thank you for this. Any longer and I think I'd have lost my mind.'

'Just don't make me regret it. Don't try to escape or hurt me. There's no way you'd get out of here in one piece without knowing the way.'

'What am I going to do?' Alfie kept his gaze on me, his eyes searching mine for answers.

'You need to give her something. Could your dad have kept the information somewhere? It's rare that people in trafficking circles don't keep dossiers on their buddies. Blackmail keeps their peers in line.'

Alfie bit his bottom lip as he pondered my question, and it sent a funny feeling into my chest. Pushing it down, I stared back at the ceiling. Was I so dejected from Harriet's rejection that I was looking for that connection in Alfie? That way only sorrow could lay. Not only was I still hopelessly in love with my unhinged beauty, but there was very little chance Harriet would let Alfie live. Even if he did, he was a millionaire with a castle. What was I? An abused orphan-turned-bodyguard with only one person in my world. A serial killer who couldn't keep her eyes off another man even when I was deep inside her.

Reaching out towards him, Alfie's breath hitched. For a long pause, we stared into one another's eyes before I broke the spell.

'I'm going to cuff you to the headboard. I'm not sure I'll sleep otherwise.' Alfie put up no protest.

Closing my eyes after securing him, I listened to the sound of his breathing until my mind turned groggy. Floating in that spot between being awake and asleep, I thought I heard him whisper, 'You don't have to sleep, there are other things I'd much rather do.'

I brushed it off as my twisted brain playing tricks on me.

TWENTY-ONE
ALFIE

Sleep weighed my eyelids as I shifted, comfort seeping into me.

Feeling warm after so many cold nights was exquisite. A heavy weight settled around my waist, and forcing my eyes open, I looked down at the thick arm circling me. Petros must have pulled me into him while we slept. The tender touch was most likely accidental, but it filled me with the first hope I'd felt since they took me. Shifting against my pillow, I turned to face him, awkwardly jerking with the way my cuffs were fixed to the headboard. The sudden motion woke him, his sleep-laced eyes blinking at me in confusion. He didn't immediately remove his arm from my stomach, almost as though he was trying the moment out for his liking.

No light entered the stone room as he rolled onto his back, my breath hitching as his hand skimmed my stomach.

'Morning,' he said, grabbing his phone from the bedside table before cursing. 'I need to go out for a bit.'

'Take me with you?'

Petros shook his head, his deep eyes roaming over my face. 'I can't. Harriet will be pissed enough to find your cage empty if she ever decides to go look. Taking you outside would have her peeling my bollocks like grapes before feeding them to me.'

The image made me clench my thighs. No, I definitely didn't want any bollock peeling action.

'I won't be long. Thirty minutes or so. I just need to go out and grab a few things.' Petros hesitated for a second, his hand halfway to reaching towards me. My pulse picked up. But then he rolled off the bed and pulled on some fresh clothes. I couldn't help but admire the deep olive expanse of his back as he changed. The defined muscles that led to his thick arms.

He left the room after grabbing his keys and phone, leaving me cuffed to the bed. A loud click sounded as he locked the door behind him.

What the hell was wrong with me? I'd gone straight to salivating over one of my captors. Logically, I knew I'd been starved of humanity for too long. Maybe I was suffering from some sort of Stockholm Syndrome or something. It was as healthy as the rest of my fucked-up sex life, to be fair. Throw me a smile, and I was on my knees and ready to worship.

Pathetic.

If I got out, I had to change things. Stop the ego-affirming one-night stands, and search for real connection. Build up friendships, hell, even tell the McGowan's how much they meant to me. *If* I made it out.

A few minutes passed while I looked around Petros' room. It was neat and fairly bare. The furniture was mismatched and scratched. Cobbled together almost. The same curved stone ceilings made up their rooms as had formed the frame of my cell. It had to be some sort of tunnel system. Aged by the look of the cast iron pipework that truncated the space.

A rattle echoed about the room, drawing my eyes to the door. A loud clanging rang out from the other side of the door, along with a feminine grunt.

What the fuck?

Wood splintered and the door swung into the room. Harriet stood, rim lit in the doorway, her chest heaving. Her hand gripped around a large wrench, which she threw onto the stone floor. It skittered to a stop near the base of the bed. Anxiety stormed through me as she neared me, her face twisting into a devilish grin.

'There you are, I thought we'd lost you.'

Her eyes grazed over my loaned jogging bottoms and the cuffs still holding me to the bed.

'So, you've managed to get to Petros, I see? I should have known he'd be fucking weak. How could he stand up to a desperate little snake like you?'

'He's spent his whole life around them, why would I be any different?' I said, hoping my words held more bluster than I had to put behind them.

'Are you insinuating that I'm a snake, Alfie?'

'I mean, if the tattoo fits.'

Her eyes closed as she inhaled deeply, her tongue darting out to trace her lower lip. 'Everything you say just makes me want to hurt you more.'

Harriet took a seat next to me on the bed before reaching into her cargo pants pocket. She produced multiple long strips of plastic, and my eyes widened as I realised they were cable ties.

I struggled as she climbed on top of me, pinning my legs with her thighs. Despite bucking like a rodeo horse, I didn't yet have the energy back to unseat her. The ties tightened around my ankles before she attached them to the footboard at the end of the bed, holding me stretched tightly.

'Let me go,' I puffed, still jerking my body beneath her.

'No.' She turned, straddling my hips. With a grin on her face, she reached into her pocket and pulled her flick knife free. Beads of sweat broke out over my body as the memory of Westley's guts flew into my mind. 'It's time to talk, Alfie.'

'I don't know anything about my dad. He slapped me on the back when I threw a sexually charged party or was caught with my dick somewhere it ought not to be. We didn't have a relationship. He never confided in me.'

'He left you his home and his wealth, are you trying to tell me that he never told you anything? Why would I believe you, liar?' She scratched the very tip of the blade along my stomach as I squirmed.

'He loved to brag. I heard him often enough. He'd tell people about how much a woman cost, and what he'd done to them. After the night of your party, I was handed around. Touched, hurt and intimidated by nameless men. He knew them well; they were comfortable together in their delinquency. He kept me for less than a week before I was sold along. I've gone back and extinguished anyone whose name I remembered. I was too late to get to see your father choke on his guts, but that group were the instigators. The ones who had women go out and recruit others under false pretences to use before making a quick profit from them.'

Harriet jutted the blade of the knife into my stomach, only shallowly, but enough to bring a well of blood to the surface, pooling around the metal.

'Fuck,' I cried out, trying to keep myself still. 'Stop. I don't know who they are.'

Her brow furrowed as she slowly removed the knife, her eyes delighting at the red path that trailed down my side. Standing, she yanked my trousers down, examining my dick. 'It's caused you and me so much pain, hasn't it?'

'Yes,' I admitted.

'I should just get rid of it. Save you the trouble of it in the future.'

'No,' I breathed. She stroked the tip of the bloodied knife over my length, it clanked against the piercings on my cock. The sensation brought my cock to life. I'd still not had release since my capture. Silently, I begged it to go. To not give her the satisfaction of being able to arouse me so easily.

My eyes widened as Harriet pulled down her combat pants, kicking them and her panties off before climbing on top of me. My dick was fully erect within seconds. I wanted to strangle the fucking thing. Even with blood oozing out of a cut on my stomach and the insane bitch standing beside me, it was still eager to please.

'How much do you think it would hurt for me to remove it?' she asked, walking her fingers up the length. Her voice was light and conversational, completely alien from the threats she was making.

'Please, just let me go. I don't have any information for you.'

'It'd be a shame not to experience those piercings before I cut your fucking dick off. This time it'll be on my terms, and the only thing you'll be excreting is blood.'

Writhing my hips, I tried to stop her, but the moment her hot cunt settled against the bulbous head of my dick, I was a goner. Her pussy lips spread as she sank down on top of me, the piercings disappearing one by own.

'Fucking hell,' she moaned, her knife-wielding hand resting against my bloodied stomach as she took what she wanted.

After the weeks of torment, she felt like fucking heaven. My eyes fluttered closed as I took a moment to just *feel*. The heat of her, the slick wetness that engulfed me. Her warm thighs against my hips.

'This is how I'm going to remember you,' she gasped as she rocked her hips. 'I'm going to replace the memory of that night with this one, seeing you bleed and struggle as I end your life, just like you ended mine all those years ago.'

The klaxons going off in my head warred with the intense pleasure she wrangled within my dick. Each arch of her hips had me on edge. By God, she looked beautiful even with the unhinged rage that filled her face. My breath hitched as she slid to the head of my dick before sinking fully back onto me, my piercings hitting her clit with every inch she stole. Her blonde hair tipped over her face as she picked up speed, and I lost all control. So close. She brought me to the edge, and I fought to hold back, believing her threats to dismember me.

Right as tears sprung, knowing I couldn't hold back any longer, she sunk her knife into my stomach, sending a shooting pain through my system. My strangled cry made her giggle as she removed her knife and stuck her finger into the small hole it left. The whole time, she kept me fully seated within her. The stabbing had chased off my orgasm until she began moving again, forcing me to descend into a mad pleasure, pain cycle.

I had no doubt she was going to kill me one way or another.

And enjoy every fucking moment of doing so.

TWENTY-TWO

HARRIET

I hated how good he felt inside me.

I hated the way he moaned as I rocked my hips, crashing my clit down over his piercings.

I loved the way his face contorted in pain every time I punched a new hole into his stomach. It took an enormous amount of restraint to only let the knife sink in a little. What I wanted was to turn him into a soppy red mess begging me to stop. But I didn't want him to die yet.

Just to suffer.

'Look at you whimpering, Alfie. Not even a knife in the gut stops you from trying to fill me up with your disgusting cum, does it?'

'No,' he groaned, his muscles contracting as I stabbed the knife into his side. Only a centimetre or so. I'd tortured enough men to know how much I could give and still let them live. Or that with one cut I could kill them outright. Knowledge was power, and I'd learned the trades of death and pleasure well.

Pressure was building between my thighs from the feeling of his thick, pierced dick spreading me open. It was a delicious sight. And hating him almost made each jolt of pleasure more heady.

'Give me a reason not to kill you, Alfie.' I shifted against him, quickening my pace as I chased down my orgasm.

'I want to help you. I don't have names, but I can help.'

Leaning over him, I held my knife to his throat, delighting in the way it trembled as he swallowed. 'Tell me how?'

Panic filled his eyes, and I felt his balls surge. Lifting myself off his dick, I laughed at the strangled cry he gave, looking down to see him fucking at the air beneath me.

'I can take you to Rosenhall,' he said through his teeth. 'We can go through his old office. I haven't touched it since he died.'

That lit a small ember inside my dark soul. At last, there was at least a possibility.

Sinking myself back down over his purpled erection, I used my knife to carve a small H across his hip. 'Tell me why I should trust you.'

My hands were red from where I used them against his seeping stomach for leverage. He hissed in pain as I quickened the pace of my hips. He looked half delirious.

'I want to make it better. What I took from you that night. I can't give it back, but I'll give you all I can. I'm sorry.'

Pushing my bloodied fingers against my clit, I gasped with the intense ripple of pleasure that shot through me. 'They all say sorry when they've got no choice. Sorry means nothing.'

Alfie's eyes pricked with tears as I dropped my knife against his chest and wrapped a hand around his throat. My clit throbbed beneath my other hand as I viciously slammed myself down on him. Each piercing thrust of his studded cock sent waves of pleasure washing through me.

'Let me prove it,' Alfie said, his words strangled by my hand on his throat.

Trusting him made me feel weak, and in a rage, I picked my knife back up and pressed it against the throbbing artery in his neck. The coppery tang of blood filled my nostrils and sweat pricked across his tattooed chest.

'I want to push this into your neck so fucking badly,' I said through a moan. 'I want to see you die without pleasure like I did the day you stole my virginity. I want to burn your fucking world down until you're left there in the ashes, broken and damned.'

My cheeks were wet with tears of humiliation as an earth-shattering orgasm ripped its way through me, sending my thoughts scattering. Waves of pleasure and shame crashed together while my cunt strangled his hard dick, my voice crying out against my will. His eyes rolled back as he jerked his hips quickly, chasing the pleasure I'd denied him. A small part of me wanted to feel him gush up inside of me, to fill my barren cunt with his treacherous seed. To complete the cycle from twenty years ago.

But he deserved to suffer. I lifted my hips from him, grinding against my hand until my pleasure was truly spent.

'Please don't stop,' Alfie said, desperation clinging to his words.

'You're lucky I'm going to let you live for another day. I'm not going to trust you, but I will let you proceed with your plan to get us into Rosenhall.'

'Will you free me after that?'

Climbing off him, I wiped my bloodied hands against the bedding before pulling my trousers back on. 'I never said I'd let you go.'

'Then why would I help you?'

Taking in his battered body, and his swollen purple dick, I considered his plight. Why indeed? Self-preservation was likely his best motivator.

'You'll help us until they are all dead. After that, I'll be finished with you.'

Alfie swallowed when I clicked my knife shut and put it in my pocket.

'And you'll let me go then?'

What was a promise between enemies? I'd done enough dark deeds for it to blight my conscience.

'Sure.'

'Harriet, what the fuck?' Anger filled Petros' words from the doorway.

Turning, I gave him a sweet smile. 'You're lucky you're not next. No one takes my toys.'

Pushing past him, a knot of shame twisted in my stomach. But he'd betrayed me. Like every other man had done.

No different from the rest.

TWENTY-THREE

PETROS

The cable ties released with a snap as I slid my knife carefully between Alfie's skin and the plastic. Hurrying, I uncuffed him before surveying the damage.

'Fuck, Alfie. I'm sorry.'

'Pretty sure it wasn't your fault.'

'I left you here like a sitting duck, so stupid!' Guilt clawed at my stomach as I lifted Alfie from the bed and took him to the bathroom. Bottles fell as I rooted through the cabinet beneath the sink. Antiseptic fell out, and I snatched up the bottle. Leaving him there, I fetched the half-used first aid kit from my room and knelt in front of him after thoroughly washing and sterilising my hands.

'I don't think she went too deep,' Alfie said while flinching as I tenderly probed around one of the cuts.

'She knows what she's doing. She's had it done to her often enough.'

Anger made my fingers tremble as I pulled out some gauze and began swabbing it over the bloody cuts. The way his breath hissed above me filled me with a level of ire for Harriet that I'd never felt before. I'd done this a hundred times over the years, picking up her battered body, cleaning it and putting it back together. We'd learned together during her captivity; the art of fixing on my part, and the art of destruction on hers.

'This will hurt,' I warned.

'It's okay,' Alfie said, closing his eyes and leaning back on the chair, his warm hands resting on my shoulders. Threading the surgical needle with a suture, I took a deep breath. It never got easier. Working methodically, I started to stitch his wounds back together, matching up the severed tattoos as best I could. They wouldn't be the neatest scars.

Alfie's fingers dug into my shoulders, yet he kept his lips pursed closed as I worked.

'I used to do this to Harriet,' I said softly, piercing the needle through his skin and pulling the edges back together. 'Her owner enjoyed knives. Loved to see how many she could take before she passed out. He'd fuck her until she woke up, then start again.'

Alfie remained tight-lipped.

'I was just a kid, really, when I was forced into his service, and saving Harriet was the one goal that kept me sane throughout the years there. We saw terrible things. She was made to do terrible things. I've long wished we could abandon this revenge mission and try to be happy, but I understand why she can't let it go. I don't think it will heal her, but not trying will kill her. It consumes her. It's been her sole goal for more than a decade.' My fingers were slippery with his blood as I worked, but stopping would make it harder for him to go back and finish.

'I love her. She's my only family. But you didn't deserve this.'

'Maybe I did,' Alfie whispered, his fingers skirting my jaw. I looked up at him as he spoke. 'I've spent years jumping from bed to bed. I've given a lot of pleasure, but I imagine I've inflicted a lot of heartache too. I've never been able to let anyone else in. Sex is the only thing I've ever been good at.'

I kept working, my mind filled with a million different thoughts. Why did his touch send electricity through me? Why did it make me feel so guilty? Alfie wasn't safe here, but getting him out would cost me my relationship with Harriet and possibly my life if she found me. Was Alfie using me? Was I using him? Pain gripped my temples, and I forced the barrage of thoughts out of my head. I had to do the one thing that felt right.

As I finished up the last suture, snipping the thread, I let out a breath. 'I'm going to take you home. Now. We need to go.'

Alfie placed a hand back on my shoulder as I made to rise, his head shaking softly. 'No. No more running. I need to make it right.'

I closed my eyes for a moment, concern darkening my thoughts. Strong fingers tipped my face upward, and I met his dark eyes.

'What can I do?' I asked.

'Make me feel human again.' Alfie's words were soft, but brimming with need.

When he pulled me towards him, I followed his urging, our lips meeting in a desperate clash of desire. He'd grown a short beard in the weeks he'd spent with us, and I ran my fingers through it, forcing the kiss to deepen as I pulled his mouth wider. The heated stroking of his tongue lit a fire deep within me. Kissing Alfie felt different to anyone I'd kissed before, like a homecoming. Like there should be a parade celebrating every single touch.

'I'm worried I'll hurt you,' I whispered, breaking the kiss and leaning our foreheads together. The way he panted against my mouth had my dick thickening against my trousers.

'I don't care.'

Wrapping him in my arms, I carried him carefully back to the bed, using one hand to push the bloodied comforter onto the floor before laying him down. My pulse quickened as I lay down next to him, feeling as nervous as I did my first time.

'I don't know how to do this... with a man,' I admitted.

'It's not very different. Just do what feels good.'

Leaning up on one elbow, I kissed Alfie again, the overwhelming desire welling up and spilling out to coat each of our desperate kisses. Careful not to touch his wounds, I let my hand trace his body, marvelling at how different each sharply toned ridge felt. When he gasped as I grazed his hips, it set a raging fire within me. What sort of magic did this tattooed hellion possess to bewitch me so thoroughly? His eyes hooded when my fingers caressed his already pulsating dick. I'd felt my own thousands of times, yet his felt completely different. Marvelling at the metal studs that graced the length of his cock, I watched his face as I circled each one.

God, he was beautiful. Even thin from a lack of proper food, and pale from too much time underground, he held an enigmatic charm that was impossible to deny. He was like a terrific magnet, pulling those near him utterly beneath his spell.

Rolling over to my bedside table brought a desperate plea from his lips. 'Please?'

Snatching a bottle of lubricant from my bedside table, I tipped a generous amount onto my hand before rolling back and pressing the wetness to him. His breath hitched as I circled the head of his cock, slowly working it over and over. His moans made me all the more desperate for him. Eagerly, I pressed my mouth to his, swallowing them down like I needed them to exist.

He arched his back as I quickened my pace, the veins in his dick like dams ready to burst.

'Fuck my face,' he gasped. 'I'm going to come otherwise.'

'Don't you want to?'

'So badly. But I want to taste you. I *need* to.'

I discarded my trousers before kneeling over him, his pretty mouth opening for me. Grazing my thumb over his lower lip, I grinned.

'Do you want my cock, Alfie?'

'Yes, fuck. Please!'

Fisting my dick, I pushed the head of it against his lips, groaning as he pressed his tongue against it, sweeping up a drop of precum.

'I should hate you,' I said as I slid my cock into his mouth. 'Harriet is everything to me, yet here I am pressing my cock into your hot little mouth.'

I let out a growl as I pressed further into his mouth, angling my hips to thrust into it like it was a cunt. His tongue kept moving with each stroke, sending waves of pleasure driving through me.

'But I can't hate you. Can I?'

He couldn't answer with my dick pumping into his mouth.

'Because I'm falling for you.'

He let out a moan that vibrated up my length and made my core tremble.

'And I will protect you from her. As I protect her from the rest of the world. I'll claim you as mine. Even if this is some wicked little ploy of yours, I'm keeping you.'

I pressed harder, slipping the head of my dick deep into his throat.

There was no resistance, and his pupils dilated as I pressed deep. God damn. I could have come right there, but I wanted more. He whimpered when I pulled out of his mouth, trying to pull me back with his fingers.

Coating my dick in the lubricant, I moved behind him, gently tipping him onto his side. With my still-slick hand, I worked my fingers against his ass, grinning at the needy whimpers he gave. Then I was there, pressing into him, becoming a part of him as I filled him up.

His entire body trembled in my arms as I slowly worked my dick into him until my hips pressed against his ass.

'Who do you belong to?' I whispered into his ear, my lips grazing his lobe.

'You.' Alfie panted, rolling his hips against me.

'I'm going to mark you as mine. Give you my cum inside this tight ass, make you spill against my fist.' I lost myself in the delirium of lust, my world compacting to nothing but that moment and how his skin slicked against my own.

'Please,' he begged, one hand reaching over his shoulder to fist into my hair. 'Fuck me.'

I needed no further volition. Pulling back, I held myself on the precipice of him, before thrusting forward as I saw stars explode. Reaching over his waist, I found his insanely erect cock and wrapped my hand around it, pumping it in time with the erratic thrusts of my hips. The pursuit of pleasure drove me, every stroke within him sending me crazy all over again. My teeth found his throat as his moans filled my ears, the salty taste of his sweat-slicked skin only making me need release all the more. I wanted to consume him. To gather up the essence that made him so enigmatic and horde it like a horny little dragon.

His cock throbbed in my hand as I quickened the furious pace on his ass. My own moans harmonised with his, reaching a crescendo as my balls tensed.

'Come for me,' I demanded through throaty grunts, his dick fucking my fist as viciously as I took his ass.

With a garbled cry, he did. Hot spurts of cum coated my hand and his stomach as I let go and filled his ass with rope after rope of my own.

'Fuck,' I groaned, blinking slowly as I cradled him against me.

Alfie began to softly sob in my arms. I didn't need to ask why. After all he'd been through, the release had to come with mixed emotions.

Grabbing a towel, I glanced towards my door, where the lock had been shattered and I hadn't even thought to close it. I thought I saw movement but disregarded it as my muddled lust-filled brain playing tricks on me. I cleaned myself and Alfie up gently before pulling him against my chest and letting him ride out his emotions.

As I rode out my own.

TWENTY-FOUR

HARRIET

The betrayal cut deep as I watched.

Petros' hands skimmed Alfie's hip as he reached for him, his dick filling Alfie. My fingernails cut into my palms, my hands fisting by my sides. It wasn't even the act of them fucking that hurt. It was the way Petros breathed Alfie in like he was an elixir. Some sort of addictive salve. Healing his wounds while it tore mine apart.

I hated the way my thighs clenched at the sight of them in their passion. The way I pictured being caught up between them, being craved by them with the ferocity in which they devoured each other. It sickened me that my desire was laced with deep, ugly jealousy. In this whole mess, they'd found each other, and I'd lost Petros.

For so many years I'd taken the fact that he'd always be there for granted. Pushed him away as a *maybe later* option. After I've got revenge. After I'd healed. I'd pushed him for so long that I'd lost my chance for an after with him. It cut me to the quick. Yet, I didn't begrudge him the intimacy. It's all he'd ever wanted. When Alfie got out and left him, it would hurt Petros terribly, and then I'd hunt Alfie down and skin him. Turn him into a motherfucking rug for hurting my partner.

The intimacy was a lie, I reassured myself. Borne out of desperation.

Their moans grew in time with their gyrating bodies, and with heat flushing my cheeks, I pushed my hand into my underwear, feeding off the thick wave of lust that washed from them. Biting my lips to silence myself, I imagined pushing Petros' hand aside and throwing my thigh over them so Alfie could fuck me. I'd had him inside me earlier, and I knew the intense pleasure that his dick could bring. As well as the intense pain.

Angry at myself, I thrust my fingers inside. Wishing I could feel their hot cum dripping from me. My own humiliation made me even wetter as I touched myself, driving myself to follow them over the edge.

Petros growled out, *come for me*, and the words unlocked my orgasm, making me use my other hand against my mouth to stifle my moan. My thighs trembled as I came with leg-quaking ferocity, Petros' words echoing in my mind again and again. It wasn't the first time I'd heard them. No, I'd often been made to come for my abusers. As though my body's reaction absolved them of their sins. As though I was a toy that could be pressed to make them laugh. I was that toy. It should horrify me to hear him say it, but it was the sort of thing I never thought could come from him. From good, sweet Petros.

I stumbled away from the doorway, tears pricking my eyes. What a fucking mess. Petros deserved someone like Alfie, not a fuck-up like me. Not someone who craved the very acts forced upon her.

Disgusting.

Unworthy.

Pathetic.

After washing my hands, I pulled out the baking ingredients, slamming them on the counter. Was it a bit crazy to make muffins when you were stressed? Maybe. But it was something I could always fall into without thinking. I didn't need to weigh or use a recipe. I remembered the ingredients and steps by rote. My mother, my sisters and I had made the same muffins every Sunday, ready for a quick breakfast before school in the week. So many times, I'd dipped into my childhood kitchen when I was suffering the worst of my torture. *One and three-quarter cups of self-raising flour.* When my back was whipped until I bled. *One teaspoon of baking powder.* When they drove knives into me while fucking me until I came. *One teaspoon of bicarbonate of soda.* When they made me strangle someone else while they filled her with their cum. *A half cup of butter...*

By the time I scooped the batter into trays, tears blanketed my cheeks.

Opening the cupboard to grab brown sugar for the topping, I paused on the bottle of poison hidden within an old mustard powder tin. My fingers grazed the yellowed tin. I could poison them both. A surge of power filled me at the thought. Making them choke and suffocate on their own blood for devouring each other's joy without me. Petros' face flashed before me, his eyes bugged and his face purple, blood seeping from his nose, mouth and ears.

Shuddering, I pushed the mustard tin away.

I sprinkled the very much regular topping onto the muffins with trembling fingers.

Would it all be worth it? The revenge. Wiping those men out had been my sole purpose for over a decade. What would drive me after? There were always more abusers to take their places.

What would I even have left?

Yes, I had my underground home, a refuge for victims and a place where I could execute the perpetrators. I had Nancy and a handful of friends who knew me for the monster I was and still didn't run. But I'd lost Petros. To my enemy.

I'd stick to the plan. Use Alfie to find out the names. Then, I'd ditch them and go on alone. As I was always meant to be.

Kill the bastards before disappearing and letting Petros move on with Alfie.

Let him have what I failed to give him.

I put the muffin tin in the oven and slammed the door closed.

Enough of the guilt and the regret.

I'm The Motherfucking Viper.

TWENTY-FIVE

ALFIE

Almost a week had passed with Petros and I holed up in his room. With each day, my wounds healed a little, and so did my broken spirit. I'd been brought to the brink of my own sanity. All of the time alone had brought my failings to the forefront of my mind. The way I ran from any form of intimacy that wasn't fleeting. The way I made space between myself and others, always flitting from place to place whenever I got too comfortable. Avoidance.

I'd spent so many years pursuing my father's pride in me that I'd never actually let myself analyse what I needed.

Petros lay next to me, his lashes dark against his olive skin. He didn't have me cuffed; I could have tried to make a bid for freedom. But I had to help Harriet into Rosenhall. I couldn't erase the past, but I could make some sort of amends to her. I could give her what she needed to find her own peace.

Between sessions of indulging in Petros' muscular body, we'd spent hours getting to know one another. There was no denying that Petros was a much better man than I. He wore his heart on his sleeve, openly telling me of his past. He didn't judge me despite the many mistakes I'd made.

I traced my fingers over his chest until he gave a sleepy smile and captured my hand with his own.

'Can't sleep?' he said in a drowsy throatiness that made my insides churn. There was nothing he did that didn't drive me mad with lust. Even after spending more time with him in the previous week than I had ever with anyone else.

'No,' I said. 'Can you tell me about this place? How did you end up down here?'

'I found Harriet sitting on top of her abuser one night, her body bathed in his blood, stabbing him repeatedly. The only clean part of her face were the tear tracks down her cheeks. I didn't doubt we'd both be buried beneath the patio when his family found us. So, I picked her up, and we ran.'

'That must have been a shock,' I said, my thumb dancing over the back of his hand.

'It was. But more than that, I was intensely proud of her. She'd suffered so much. For years. If she hadn't lashed out, I didn't doubt they would have killed her. Before we left, I had to cut the tracker out of her neck, the scar remains just below her ear. She didn't even flinch when I did it.' Petros turned to face me, keeping a hold on my hand.

'We didn't know where to go. She didn't feel like she could return to her family. She was too traceable. The others would have tracked her down and taken her. Or killed them all.'

'She has a family?' They must have long thought her dead but must have stayed in limbo for a long time. It sent a pang of guilt through me. She'd been dragged from her life for me. I may not have asked for it, but I was the catalyst who started her whole terrible journey.

'I've checked in on them once or twice without letting her know. Just in case she ever wants to go back. Her father sadly passed not long after she left, but her mother still lives in the same house in Manchester. Her sisters have children and partners, and it looks like they've managed to move on from her disappearance.' Petros' eyes glazed a little as he spoke.

'So home wasn't an option?'

'No, and my family are gone. We took to the streets. Stealing food. Begging. Fighting. Eventually, we met her friend Nancy, who spoke of someone who had a place we could call home. They showed us to this disused bunker system. It became our refuge. As the months passed, I thought Harriet would begin to heal, but she didn't. There was too much harm done. It festered and with it, her anger grew.'

I took Petros' hand to my lips and grazed his knuckles with a kiss. The urge to spill my affection on him was overwhelming. Usually, after sleeping with someone, I had a gut reaction to flee.

'One day while fetching supplies, Harriet saw a man trying to force himself on one of the homeless women she knew. Without hesitation, she slit his throat. She took the woman in and offered what little we had to help her get back on her feet. Harriet saw her purpose for the first time. Eventually, rumours spread, and she got tips about people higher and higher in society. Wives who were terrified of their husbands, but knew they lacked the power to see justice. Donations came piling in as word spread. Someone was finally doing what the powerful abusers were doing, skirting around legality. She took on the name *Viper* for her propensity to use poison. The tattoos on her back didn't erase the damage inflicted on her, but it let her claim it back on her terms.'

'And you loved her through it all?'

Petros' eyes shone as he nodded. 'I can't do anything but love her.'

'It's okay. It makes you the man you are.'

'What if I can't choose?' Petros' voice quaked, and he closed his eyes.

'Humans don't have a finite amount of love. Loving her doesn't mean you can't fall in love with me.' Even voicing it sounded crazy. Who could possibly love *me*?

'I know. I'm already deep down the rabbit hole with you.'

'Is that a euphemism?' I asked, lightening the moment.

'It can be,' he laughed, pulling me against him, and letting me lose myself in his arms.

TWENTY-SIX

HARRIET

The two of them were sickening me. Wrapped up together like two happy little bunnies during mating season. I kept telling myself it was Petros' betrayal that made me feel so bitter, but the green vines of envy were choking me with each passing moment.

Every contented sigh or desire-fuelled moan sent me looking for an escape. From my own home!

Petros had warned me not to touch Alfie again, and I'd stuck by it, touching myself instead to the sound of Petros' headboard in the depths of the night. Shame fuelled my lust even as I wallowed in my hatred of Alfie.

I couldn't bring myself to hate Petros, no matter how hard I tried. He'd suffered, at my side as much as anywhere else. I'd looked past him, forever expecting him to remain by my side. To be there when I was ready.

But could I ever be ready to give him what Alfie did? To open up to him and let him in?

Not when I knew I didn't deserve his adoration. That I used it to spur me on, but I knew I didn't deserve it.

I could take no more.

I stood in front of Petros' door and rapped against it with a tight fist.

He pulled it open a few moments later, looking more relaxed than I'd ever seen him. The tension across his jaw was gone, and he leaned against the door frame looking at me.

'Yes?'

How times had so quickly changed. Pre-Alfie, he would have been ready to follow me at the drop of a hat.

'We need to go to Rosenhall. Alfie is well enough by the sounds of it.'

Alfie relaxed back against the headboard, his tattooed chest bare, and Petros' jogging bottoms bunched around his hips.

'Have you been listening to us, Harriet?'

A white-hot flash of anger flared, and I fought to keep it at bay, ignoring his remark entirely.

'I'm serious. I'm done waiting. If you guys aren't ready to leave your cum hole then I'll go myself.'

I turned to leave, but Petros' warm hand reached out and took my arm gently. The tender touch almost broke me.

'Wait. You're right. We can't keep putting it off,' Petros said.

Snatching my arm away like he'd scalded me, I turned to face them.

'What day is it?' Alfie asked, standing up from the bed and making the sweatpants sink dangerously low on his hips. Each step made them slip a little further. I couldn't tear my eyes away. His stomach and chest were still littered with fresh red scars. I didn't know what affected me more— lust or guilt.

'It's Monday, why?'

'The staff usually have the day off on Tuesdays. Grieves will be there, but if you want the best chance of sneaking in without being apprehended, it's then.'

'Will this Grieves call the police?' It won't be a problem to silence him.

'No. I don't think so. He's the one who practically raised me. I trust him more than anyone else. Pretty much.' He took a quick glance at Petros before a pink tinged his cheeks.

Fucking barf.

'I sure hope you're right. I won't have anyone sabotage this. Not you and your lying tongue, and not some aged butler either.'

'It'll be okay,' Petros said. He looked like he was about to reach out and pull me into his arms like he used to. I used to hate it. The pity drove me insane. But now, I craved his strong arms reassuring me more than ever. His arm froze in hesitation before dropping back to his side. Another dagger to my heart.

He'd found someone more worthy of his love than me.

Who could blame him?

'Tomorrow evening, then,' I said before leaving them to their happiness. Needing to get into Rosenhall was the only thing stopping me from sneaking in and cutting their miserable cocks off in the night.

TWENTY-SEVEN

PETROS

Alfie looked back to himself in his laundered clothing. It was almost odd to see him outside my room, dressed like he had been the night Harriet and I took him. So much had changed.

I packed my knife and slid a gun into the holster at my waist before concealing it under my jacket. When I turned around, Alfie was wolfing down one of Harriet's muffins from the kitchen counter.

'No,' I said, lunging for it and knocking it from his hand. Crumbs coated his lips.

'What was that for?' Came his mumbled reply as he swallowed down a mouthful.

Panic swirled in my stomach. I'd push my fingers down his goddamned throat if I needed to. Before I had the chance, Harriet's laughter rang out behind me.

'No need for dramatics. I haven't poisoned him. Yet, anyway,' she said, rolling her eyes.

'That's the best fucking muffin I've ever tasted. Holy fuck, you can bake.' Alfie yoinked another from the countertop and tucked in.

My heart was thundering ten to the dozen. I placed my hands on the counter and took a few slow breaths. The strength of feeling I had for him was threatening to drown me.

Alfie made his way back to the room, happy as Larry with his muffin in hand.

'How could you do it?' Harriet said in a low voice.

'Do what?'

'Choose him over me. After everything.' The fact that hurt was evident in her voice sent sharp pains through me. I'd never wanted to hurt her.

'He paid for what he did. I offered to get him out before you killed him.' Harriet's brow furrowed, the corners of her mouth pulling downward. 'You nearly killed him. He's not the devil you think he is. I promise. He reminds me an awful lot of you, actually.'

'Broken?' she said, anger barbing the word.

'Strong. Resilient. Just.'

'He told me you loved me.'

'I love you. Not past tense. It was always you.' Turning towards her, I reached out and threaded her fingers into mine. She tensed up but didn't pull away.

'It's not me now. I was only good enough until you found someone better.'

'You didn't want me,' I said. Putting the words out into reality hurt.

'I just needed to take care of the demons who haunted me first. I didn't believe that you could truly love me, not romantically. Every look was always filled to the brim with pity.' Her eyes searched mine.

'It was never pity.'

'But now you have Alfie. Broken, but he can give you everything on a platter that I can't.' Why had she waited so long to tell me that there truly had been feelings on her part? 'I thought you'd always be here with me.'

'I will.' Somehow.

'Do you think he's going to want to stay down here forever? Living beneath the real world while we kill people? He's a millionaire, Petros. He's not one of us. He hasn't lived the life we have.' Her words were still laced with anger.

'I don't know how it will work.'

'You'll leave me. You'll go and live in his playboy mansion with him. I'll be nothing but a deranged memory.'

'Harriet,' I whispered, pulling her to me and setting my mouth over hers. She opened her lips and kissed me, but the slide of her tongue was coated with sadness. The touch of her skin against my hands felt like a goodbye rather than a hello.

I pulled away; our faces still close. Her eyes flashed with an unreadable emotion.

'After we go to Rosenhall, I'm going ahead on my own. After I have the information, you can go. Be with him. Live a normal life.' I grazed my thumb over her cheek as she spoke, each word as much of a wound as she'd inflicted on Alfie.

'No, Harriet I don't want that.'

'You made your bed. And I get it. Truly. I'll leave the two of you alone as soon as I have the list in my hands.'

Turning her head, she moved away from my hand. The same coldness I'd seen so many times before settled over her face, pulling her into the mask that she wore as the Viper. The one that said *I'll burn the whole fucking world.*

The mask had never been for me before.

TWENTY-EIGHT

HARRIET

Nancy waited outside my door, leaning against the wall. I'd gone out to get a bit of space from the lovebirds.

'Sorry,' I said, 'I didn't hear you knock.'

'I didn't.' She gave me a soft smile. 'I was walking past, and all sorts of bad auras were leaking from inside. I stopped to make sure you were okay.'

I was too exhausted with Alfie and Petros' nonsense to argue about her auras.

'Your prisoner has changed sides?' she asked as I leaned back against the stone wall beside her, glad of her presence even with her mumbo jumbo.

'Petros has.' I almost spat the words out.

'Mm,' she responded before reaching between us and softly squeezing my hand. Her touch made emotion well up my throat, and I worked hard to force it back. I squeezed her back, too. 'Harriet, sometimes plans change, and you have to stop fighting the changes. Good can come from a bad thing. It's not always an easy path to navigate, but don't close yourself off from it. If Petros means as much to you as I think he does, fight for him.'

'It's too late. Alfie's got him under his spell.'

'There's a good chance it's just lust. Or his need to mend broken things. He might well turn sour on Alfie when there isn't the forbidden aspect. How many men marry their mistress only to find that it was the risk of being with her that they loved?'

'So, I'm just supposed to sit and wait for him to get bored and come back to me? That's pathetic.'

'He hasn't left you, love. Not yet. If you push him away he will.' Nancy's fingers were cold against mine.

'And what about Alfie?'

'If you can't kill him, maybe try and see what Petros sees in him. After all, he's fallen for you both.'

I swallowed down the lump in my throat as the door opened behind me. Standing up straight, I gave Nancy's hand a final squeeze before she slunk off.

Petros and Alfie came out of the open door, Alfie looking almost panicked to be going into the real world again.

'You ready?' Petros said. I wasn't sure to whom.

'I am,' Alfie and I said in unison. I couldn't help but glare at him.

'If you double cross me, or your butler alerts the authorities, I won't hcsitate to kill you both before using your bodies to start a bonfire that will burn your precious castle down.' Alfie didn't flinch at the threat.

With a smirk, he replied, 'I'd be disappointed in you if you didn't.'

Smug little wanker.

The thought brought an image of his glorious fucking cock, and I was left leading the way out, mad at myself.

It's just a cock.

A stupid, ugly cock.

I didn't want it.

The waterfall in my underpants called me a fucking liar.

TWENTY-NINE

ALFIE

Petros pulled the old banger of a car into the little clearing in the forest down a rarely-used back path. My ass ached from the long ride from Glasgow. Rosenhall was deep in the Highlands, and we'd been on the road for hours. More than anything, I wanted a cup of tea and a sit-down, not a clandestine mission in my own home.

We got out and traipsed through the woods, the tension of being stuck together in the car not reducing despite the expanse of the woods around us.

The walls were a sight for sore eyes when they veered into view. However much I'd struggled with my childhood with my adoptive father, Rosenhall had always held a magic for me. Fighting make-believe monsters in the woods with sticks. Exploring the lesser-used areas of the house before it had been turned into the extensive hedonistic retreat it now was. Before the spa, the basement had housed boxes and boxes of forgotten delights that childhood me had adored.

Without my father inside, the castle greeted me like an old friend.

Harriet's hand grasped my arm briefly before she snatched it back with a wide-eyed look. Clearing her throat, she carefully pressed a glare back into her features. 'No funny business. I swear to God, I'll—'

'Yeah,' I said, starting back up towards the house. 'You'll sever my bollocks and feed me them. Or skin me and stuff me like an oversized teddy bear. Or bite me with your venomous little mouth. I get it.'

Petros snorted beside me before coughing to try and hide his reaction.

Harriet grumbled behind me but kept following regardless.

'I should go in first,' I said. 'In case there's something on.'

'There's hardly a car in sight and no noise. We go in together.' Harriet pushed past me, forest floor foliage crackling beneath her boots. She hovered as we reached the paved area to the side of the house.

'This way.' I led us towards the back entrance, hoping the staff entrance still had the same keycode.' Otherwise, I'd need to get Grieves out of his bed by knocking on the front door. Ideally, I'd get them in and out with the bloody list Harriet craved so badly without anyone noticing.

The steel buttons were cold against my fingertips. I punched in the last working code I knew. Red light.

'Fuck,' I whispered.

Taking a deep breath, I closed my eyes and thought back. The staff codes always worked in a pattern. The numbers on the outside cycled upward each week, while the numbers in the middle cycled down. They were changed weekly. I had no idea how long I'd been gone. My last visit to Rosenhall was a month before they took me. I'd used the staff entrance to sneak in, so the partying guests wouldn't drag me into a sex game, as they so often did.

'How long have I been with you guys?' I asked.

Petros audibly swallowed before answering, 'Eight weeks.'

Fuck. I'd been missing for two whole months?

The last code had been *two-seven-nine-one*. Closing my eyes, I tried to imagine a bike lock, the numbers shifting as I counted. My brain felt like mush after weeks of barely using it for anything but wallowing in pity.

'Four,' I said. 'Remember that.'

I kept cycling the numbers.

'Four Five Seven Three.'

I hoped.

I keyed in the code and held my breath at the delay. Green. We were in. With apprehension prickling at my skin, I opened the door. Silence awaited.

We closed the door behind us, and Harriet pulled out a tiny torch, lighting up the rooms I knew so well. I'd spent almost as much time in the staff areas as I had in the house. The chefs and cleaners doted on me and showed me what kindness could be in a home devoid of it. I almost wished they were there to greet us. I wanted them to know I wasn't dead in a ditch somewhere.

Making our way silently into the main part of the house, I froze as soft music floated from one of the large living rooms. I sincerely hoped that Grieves had just forgotten to turn it off. The rich jazz music floated towards us, increasing in volume the closer we got to the doorway. Trying to walk as silently as possible, we crept past, only daring to breathe as we neared the end of the corridor.

The smooth bannister was cool beneath my palm as I led them up the stairs, all of us pausing as a step creaked beneath Petros' feet.

My own pulse thrummed in my ear as we waited, listening intently. Bar the far-off music, there was nothing.

Rounding the stairwell, we reached the landing. Almost there. I hadn't been in Dad's office for years. His business affairs had largely gone digital before I took over, and his slew of accountants, lawyers, and dodgy fuckers kept it all running smoothly for me.

'Alfie, duck!' Came an angry voice from behind us. Turning, I was staring directly down the business end of a shotgun.

I held my hands up in front of me. 'Grieves, it's okay.'

'You've been missing for two fucking months.' The pain was palpable as he spoke. Warmth filled me.

Harriet made to move beside me, but I stopped her with a hand. 'Don't you fucking dare. He's one of mine.'

Grieves lowered the barrel half an inch, his sparse hair dishevelled. I don't think I'd ever seen him in any state of anything less than perfection. Pushing the gun down, I threw my arms around his neck. He still smelled like Old Spice, and the scent threw me right back into childhood. Into him patching scraped knees and telling me off for stealing cakes from the kitchen before a party. Into him teaching me how to shave and wear a suit correctly.

'God, I've missed you,' I whispered against his ear. When he pulled back to scrutinise me, I was glad I'd taken the time to shave.

'Where the hell have you been?'

'A little tied up,' I said with a smile, shrugging a shoulder. Petros snorted again.

'Did they take you?' he asked.

'You know me, forever unreliable Alfie.'

Grieves' eyebrows lowered. 'Not with me. You've never been unreliable with me. We've had the McGowans hunting for you, the police searching everywhere that had even a tenuous link to you. You disappeared without a trace.'

I held his upper arms lightly with my hands. 'I'm sorry I made you worry. I'm helping these friends of mine with something, but I need to ask a huge favour of you. I need you not to tell a single soul that you saw me. I'm still missing, okay? Only for a little while longer, and then I'll be back.'

I daren't look at Petros as I said it lest I saw any hurt in his face.

'I need the key to Dad's old office, and an hour or two.'

It was a lot to ask of an ageing friend. His eyes darted between Harriet, who continued to look like she might stab him if he merely breathed at her wrong, and Petros who towered behind me. They definitely didn't look like my usual rich trust fund and mafia friends.

'Promise me you'll come back.' Grieves' voice trembled with emotion. 'Promise it.'

'I promise.'

'You,' Grieves said to Harriet. 'You promise. Promise me you'll bring him back very soon.'

Harriet looked almost surprised to be addressed by the shotgun-wielding butler. For sure, I thought she'd refuse, but something in her eyes softened just a fraction.

'I promise.'

Grieves stared at us for another minute, his mouth drawing into a thin line. 'I'll be back with the key.'

THIRTY

HARRIET

We continued on towards the office, passing room after room. Turning near the top of another staircase, we walked through an open space with vaulted ceilings. Throughout the space, opulent couches were interspersed with antique tables. One particular table stood out, its edges inlaid with mother-of-pearl.

A wave of nausea washed over me as I stood rooted to the spot, the table launching me into a torrent of pain.

They'd pinned me to that table. After Alfie had used me and stumbled off without another care. My thighs tensed at the memory of their hands forcing my thighs wide, at the decorative table cold beneath my slippery tears. At begging for them to stop. To let me go.

Their laughter as one removed his belt and whipped my thighs while another forced himself into my mouth. A knife at my throat in case I dared fight back.

'Harriet.' Petros' soft voice broke through my reverie, stealing me from the pain long enough for me to take a shaky breath in.

A body shifted near the archway at the far end of the room, Alfie's pale face watched me, and I hated that he saw how much being there affected me. He and Grieves left the room after passing a look towards Petros.

The rug beneath the table was different. Had they changed it when I had bled too much?

Count the strokes, you little whore. We're going to destroy that pathetic cunt tonight. The memory of coming against one of their dicks, humiliation storming through me as my body betrayed me. Their glee in it. It's why they decided to keep me rather than kill me. An amusement. A toy.

Strong arms looped around me, pulling my face against Petros' expansive chest.

'It's okay,' he murmured into my hair, his hot breath comforting me, bringing me back into the present and away from the ghastly memories that had felt more real than they had in many years. 'They aren't here. You are safe with me. I won't let them hurt you ever again.'

My fingers shook as I knitted them behind his back, tucking my face in tightly to him as my emotions turned me this way and that.

'You are going to kill every last one of them. They will suffer under your hands.' Petros' words were filled with anger—anger on my behalf. How had I overlooked him for so many years?

'You are the best friend I've ever had,' I whispered, pulling back a fraction to look at him. Wetness skirted my eyelashes as he smiled down at me.

'You've been my everything since the day I walked into that room all those years ago. The sun to my shadow.'

'Oh Petros, if anyone's the sun, it's you.' His deep umber eyes searched my face, and his breath hitched. Standing up on my tiptoes, I brushed my lips over his. It was the softest touch, barely a kiss at all, yet the feeling behind it hit me in the gut more than any other had.

His hands moved up into my hair, cupping my face. 'Harriet, I love you. I have done forever.'

There was a hint of something pained beneath the words, the declaration tainted. By something. By someone.

'But you love him more,' I whispered.

'No. Not more. But I'm growing to adore him too. And I don't know how to navigate this. All of that can wait, though. We need to put this chapter of your story to bed.'

'To the grave,' I said.

Petros nodded, scooping me against his chest again. 'Stay here with us.

The demons from your past are clawing at you, determined to drag you into despair. Don't let them. If you need me to ground you, grab my hand. I'll protect you from them like I did from the devils who hurt you.'

'Thank you.'

Taking my hand, he led me through the room, away from the table and the atrocities inflicted on me there.

Towards our next stage.

We caught up with Alfie as Grieves unlocked the door before handing him the key.

'It's still untouched?' Alfie asked, his face set in a hard mask we'd so rarely seen him employ. Usually, he preferred using his smart mouth to get through a situation. I wondered if his memory demons clawed at him too.

Grieves nodded. 'Not a soul has set foot in there like you asked when he passed.'

'Thank you,' Alfie said. 'Go and get yourself a cup of tea, I'll return the key when we're finished.'

The older man looked reluctant to leave Alfie with us, his face turning into a frown when he looked us over. After a moment, he nodded before dipping his head at us and taking his leave.

By the time he was out of view, Petros let out a low whistle. 'Can't believe you grew up here. This place is insane.'

'A gilded cage,' Alfie said, pulling his shoulders back and taking a breath. Reluctance rolled from him like waves hitting the shore, yet still he depressed the door handle and opened his own personal hell. For me. Nancy had said to look for what Petros saw in him, and that little act of self-sacrifice made me see it. I may have forced him to help me, but Petros had offered him and out, and he stayed to help me, even when I hated him.

Soft lighting illuminated the room when Alfie flipped the switch. The office was fairly big, the walls lined with hundreds of old books and not a single one looked like it was from the past century. An ornate desk stood proudly in the centre of the room, the only non-library wall behind it covered in ornate panelling. The wall had two portraits hanging, and a gap where one seemed to have been previously.

'He removed me,' Alfie said when he saw me staring. 'Smashed it to pieces after one particular disappointment on my part. The others are his wife, my adoptive mother, and him.'

Turning his back to the pictures, he started pulling open drawers on the desk and rifling through paperwork. Thick dust wafted on the top of the desk as he placed pile after pile of paper onto it. Petros scanned the shelves of books, while I made my way to a cabinet and paused with my fingers on one of the drawer knobs. My breath caught in my throat.

'You can open it,' Alfie said. 'I promise he's long dead.'

The fact he'd noticed my discomfort made me feel weak, and I used that to prod me into action. Pulling the drawer open, I leafed through its contents. What looked like ledgers for repayments for different companies. Nothing of note. Another held long dried-out cigars and their paraphernalia. The next cupboard hid an aged whisky collection, most of the bottles half empty. Shit, some of them were older than my grandparents would be. That sneaky reminder of my past hit me like a punch. Would they ever still be alive?

'There's nothing here,' Alfie said, his voice tight. He'd truly hoped to find what I needed.

'There has to be.' It couldn't be the end. Not when I was finally so close.

Petros was by my side as I picked up one of the whisky bottles and took a deep draw of the amber liquid. I winced at the burn against my throat.

'That might not be very drinkable,' Petros said. Stating the bleeding obvious.

'It's still alcohol.' I replied before taking another swig, coughing as the fiery burn scorched my insides.

'Fuck it, agreed.' Alfie grabbed a bottle and swallowing a monstrous gulp before letting out a hiss.

I gave him a small smile as he rested back against the dusty desk and chinked our bottles together. 'We'll keep looking. There has to be something somewhere. Can you remember anything about any of them?'

'They all had a small tattoo of a curled fox on them. Your dad included. Their faces are blurry. They used me on and off for a few weeks before I was sold off into the system. The faces of those who came after jumble in my head with the ones who came before. Those were the faces I got to see. Some would wear hideous masks. But they all had the tattoo.'

Petros pressed a hand against my shoulder, squeezing with reassuring warmth. 'We'll find something. With the ridiculous size of this place, there has to be something somewhere. Would your friend Grieves know about your dad's associates?'

Alfie shrugged. 'He might, but unless the tattoos were large or visible, he likely wouldn't have noticed them. He never really got up close with the guests. His job was to manage, not to join in. My father has a lot of acquaintances, hundreds of people have come here to play. The people who are into the shady side of sex might well not be people who partook in the consensual games. Consent has always been such an open and integral part of Rosenhall's history.'

I let my cheek rest against Petros' hand and closed my eyes. Goosebumps coated my arms as apprehension filled my stomach. We needed something.

Anything.

THIRTY-ONE

PETROS

Harriet's cheek was warm against my fingers, and it felt like some sort of truce had descended between the three of us. Alfie's face was filled with disappointment at the lack of anything in his father's office.

Was the whole trip for nothing? Harriet and I had been working to get to that moment for so long, could it really have been for nothing?

There had to be more. Poking Alfie when he was clearly already feeling so conflicted at being under the ghost of his deceased father would be cruel. Hurting him was the last thing I wanted to do. But Harriet needed names. My loyalties between them were divided, and it was shredding my heart to have to push either of them.

An ancient clock lay silent on the wall, stopped in time from neglect. Like both of their memories were.

'Harriet, were you ever in this office?'

She took another look around, her eyebrows knitting as she threw her mind back to a time she'd rather forget. A shudder made her shoulder move beneath my hand. 'No, never here.'

My focus fell back to Alfie.

'You must have been in here before. Is there anything you can remember? A hidden safe? Secret desk drawer? Anything at all that might help us?' I spoke softly, melting as his dark lashed eyes met my face.

'I was in here often when I was little, but rarely as a teen or adult.'

'Why?' I asked, trying to probe just a little further. Trying to jog something from the recesses of his memories.

'I pissed him off once. He dragged me out of his office and beat me. I coughed up blood over the wall in the corridor. He made me scrub it off even with a wrist I couldn't bend.' If I could have reached into the cosmos and killed his father's spectre, I would have. Clenching my teeth together, I tried to go just a little further, feeling like a total cunt for doing so.

'Why was he so mad?' I asked. 'What pushed him so hard?'

'It was so long ago...' Alfie said with a wince, trailing off as he closed his eyes and took a shaky breath. Emotion squeezed in my chest as Harriet reached out and threaded her fingers through Alfie's, giving him support she so rarely gave willingly. My eyes misted, and she put down her whisky bottle, reaching out and taking my hand too.

Alfie looked lost in his reverie for a few minutes, his thumb relentlessly flicking over the tip of one of Harriet's fingers. His whole body thrummed with tension, the tendons in his neck fraught.

'I'd been playing hide and seek. He'd had friends over who had children with them. Other children in Rosenhall were a rare occurrence. We'd spent the day playing outside and sneaking into the kitchens, pinching food made for whatever dinner they had planned. One of the others had suggested hide and seek. I'd found my dad's office unlocked and decided it was the perfect spot. I still remember my heart racing while I hid myself beneath the desk. Eventually, apprehension had turned to boredom as time passed without any sight of the other kids.'

He closed his eyes again, looking like he was flicking through index cards long covered in dust within his head.

'I'd found a circular button with a raised texture on it beneath the desk. Curiosity had me playing with it, hoping that a secret compartment drawer would appear, maybe stuffed with sweets I could have shared with my new friends. It didn't do anything. What seemed like only a moment later, my dad tore into the room and dragged me from under the desk, screaming bloody murder at me.'

Alfie let go of Harriet's hand as he wrapped his arms around himself. 'I remember being surprised that the buttery, soft leather shoes could hurt so much when he kicked me.'

Moving to stand in front of Alfie, I held him in my arms, hoping to give as much comfort to that poor inner child as the man before me.

'You didn't deserve that,' I said, pressing my lips into his hair. 'He didn't let himself know the amazing person you are. Moulding you into another version of him was never going to work because you are so much more than he ever could have been.'

Alfie's arms tightened around my stomach, returning the squeeze I gave him. He cleared his throat and briskly ran his hands over his eyes before pushing up off the desk to stand. 'Guess we should check if it's still there.'

THIRTY-TWO

ALFIE

I hated being in his office. It was like he was there, hovering over me, all of his anger and disapproval suffocating me with each passing minute. Had it been a mistake to come?

The button hadn't done anything that day, not as far as I could remember. It was probably just a stupid childhood notion that there was even a button.

Glancing at Harriet's hopeful face, I felt like a prize dick. I shouldn't have gotten their hopes up. It was all beginning to feel like a wild fucking goose chase.

I crouched in front of the desk and peered underneath, the memory of that day flooding through me. The excitement and joy. The fear and pain. Grieves had slept on a fold-out bed in my room for weeks, helping me to heal. Maybe even as a protection from my own father. I owed that man so much more than I had ever given him.

'Can I borrow your torch?' I asked Harriet, who handed it over without a peep.

Moving a little further under the desk, it felt a million times smaller than it had back then. I searched the rich, old wood for any sign of the button.

There it was. At the upper back corner, a small wooden knob with a golden pattern rising from its curved surface. Inching closer, I flashed the light over the surface, a sharp intake of breath echoing from my own mouth.

'What is it?' Petros asked from behind me.

'It's here. And the pattern is a tiny fox cub.'

Before I could move, Harriet was forcing herself into the tiny space beside me, peering at the golden symbol. The small squeak that left her throat gave me all the confirmation I needed. Fuck, it was all true. My father had had plenty of failings. His anger, his hatred of me, his underhand dealings as part of the Scottish criminal underworld. But I'd never suspected him of the terrible things he'd done to Harriet. And others? Nausea bubbled up in my gut.

Harriet reached up and pressed the button. It moved, but nothing happened.

'Has anything changed around the office?' I said, raising my voice to reach Petros.

Footsteps echoed beyond the desk.

'Can't see anything.'

'It has to do something,' Harriet replied, bashing it harder. Twisting it. Finally pulling it. With the pulling, a loud click echoed through the room.

'Holy shit,' Petros whispered. We scrambled to dislodge ourselves from beneath the desk. Harriet's elbow connecting with my side.

Standing up, I took stock of the office. Almost nothing had changed from my point of view. Harriet manhandled my shoulders, turning me to face the wall with my missing portrait. Right behind where my face had been hung, the panelling had swung open revealing a dark space behind it.

Inching forward, I held up the torch. Apprehension brought my neck out in a clammy sweat as I pressed my hand against the cold wood, opening it fully. Using the small beam of light, I found a light switch on the wall behind the opening, flicked it, and illuminated the space.

A bed stood in the middle of the room, a series of chairs facing it in all directions. Mirrors hung on two of the walls meaning, that no matter where you sat, you had multiple views of the bed. A shower filled one corner, and a bar the other. Behind the bar there was another door, not at all hidden.

Harriet stood frozen; her face twisted into pure fear. After seeing her as the unflappable femme fatal, it was a harrowing vision.

'You know this place.' There was no question in Petros' words.

'Yes,' she whispered, her fingers clenching against the hem of her top. The fabric bunched in her hands. I hated seeing her like that. It was worse than seeing her slaughter a man like a farm animal. 'I spent a long time in this room. I didn't know it was in Rosenhall though. I woke up here after passing out. I thought they'd moved me.'

'We can search in here if you need to go get some air outside,' I offered.

'I don't want to be on my own,' she admitted, shrinking into a corner, her arms crossing over her stomach.

'We'll be quick,' Petros said.

There was little in the room except the furniture, so I made my way across the room and opened the other door. Inside was a neat little space with a load of lockers, some benches and a toilet cubicle. It wouldn't have been out of place in a home gym. Hell, maybe that's what it had been built as.

But one filing cabinet stood out like a sore thumb. The drawers were stiff with disuse but begrudgingly gave way under force. A number of brown manilla folders lay within each of them. Opening them revealed details of various men and women. Names, ages, and known family members. Pictures too. Smiling at the camera or beaten and teary. Clothed and sitting on my father's knee. Naked and degraded. Fury had the folders creasing between my fingers as Petros and Harriet joined me. I handed the file back and heard Harriet gasp. This is what she had been searching for. Real, solid proof.

File after file hit me with fresh waves of anger and revulsion. My life had been built on this absolute hell. For my father to have been involved, there would be more behind it than coercive sex, he had all the sex he could ever have needed. It had to be about more. About power, or money.

'We should turn these over to the police,' I said, opening another drawer and feeling broken with each new face that greeted me within the files. 'They can track them down, give their families either hope or at least a conclusion.'

'It's too late,' Harriet replied. 'They'll either be dead or gone. The men like your father don't hold onto them. They have their fun and sell them on. These guys are bulletproof. Their friends are lawyers, judges and police chiefs. At maximum, they might do a few years. Most likely, they wouldn't even suffer an inconvenience from an investigation. It would be quashed quicker than a bug beneath their boot.'

A heavy file was the last in the drawer I was looking through, and opening it sent a dagger to my heart. Harriet was younger, but the pretty face in the bar was unmistakably her. Then there were pictures. So many fucking pictures. One caught my eye because I recognised my younger self behind her. Partially slumped over her back, my eyes were unfocused and bleary. The camera was primarily on her face, her tears visible and her mouth contorted in a forever-frozen cry. My father's hand was on the back of her head, pinning her down to the pearl-clad table.

'I'm so sorry,' I whispered, closing the file and handing it to Harriet. She didn't open it.

Sickened at my younger self, I opened the final drawer. Photo after glossy photo filled it. Each one showed a man in an uncompromising situation with someone from the other files, showing them very clearly enjoying hurting people. At the bottom of the drawer lay a tiny notebook embossed with the same fox symbol. Inscribed in my father's neat handwriting were names, locations, and crimes. Each page was for a different man, headshots pasted into the corners.

There were a dozen. Some had dark inky crosses blocking out their page. Six remained.

'Do you recognise them?' I asked Harriet, looking up as she leaned over my shoulder for a better view.

'All of them.'

THIRTY-THREE

HARRIET

The folder felt like it weighed a thousand pounds as I carried it back through the castle, the little notebook clutched tightly against it. All those years, I'd sat sandwiched in a drawer with the others. I hadn't realised that returning to Rosenhall would affect me so thoroughly. The hidden room had torn me apart, sending ripples of anxiety coursing through me. Nothing good had ever come from that despicable cell.

Until now.

As much as being there had set old wounds seeping afresh, I'd claimed the power back in that room. It wasn't only a place of tragedy. I had one small victory over it. I had their names. I had evidence that was irrefutable. We'd shut the other files back in the hidden room, leaving them for Alfie to deal with later when we'd decided the best course of action. Not until after those six men were dead.

We neared the end of the corridor, and Alfie paused ahead of us.

'We can double back on ourselves and take the fire exit stairs,' he said. They'd both seen my reaction to the room, the intense power it still held over me.

I hated that anything could throw me back to that scared, defenceless girl I had been. I wasn't her anymore.

'No,' I said, striding forward and brushing past Alfie. 'It's fine.'

Beyond the emotional devastation, the room was beautiful. The double-height ceilings had an ornate oval window covered in stained glass roses and thorns. Rich reds tangled with the barbed greens high above me. I'd never noticed them that night. I had barely been able to see through my tears.

I relinquished my files onto the mantelpiece and faced the room, breathing in long, ragged breaths. The memories swam at the edge of my vision, vying for attention like dark little wraiths. I needed to vanquish them.

'I need to force the memories out,' I muttered, as much to myself as anyone else.

'You can't,' Petros said. He came to stand beside me, his fingers resting against my waist.

'You can replace them with new ones.' Alfie stood at my other side, and I tipped my face at his words. 'You can replace them with ones where you control what happens. Where you are the person in charge. Where no one can hurt you.'

My pulse picked up in my throat at the nearness of both of them, their body heat close enough to warm me.

'I can go and leave you two to make better memories here,' Alfie said, reaching out and grazing a finger over my forearm.

Petros cleared his throat to talk, but I spoke before he could continue. 'No. You two have your own thing, and I can't force myself between that. Petros doesn't owe me anything. I don't need his pity.'

'It's never been pity,' Petros said, cupping my chin and pulling me around to him. 'You are the strongest person I know. I've watched you suffer through some of the worst things that can happen to a person, and you came out swinging. Even then, you didn't run or hide. You hunt down the fuckers who hurt other people. You became their saviour, and you never asked for anything in return. I don't pity you, Harriet. I worship you.'

A lump grew in my throat as he spoke. Everything suddenly became crystal clear.

'I love you so fucking much,' I whispered, standing on my tiptoes and pressing my lips to his. He poured all of his love, finally requited, into his kiss. My fingertips pushed up over his shoulders and into his

hair as I finally let go of it all. The hurt, the anger, the crushing weight
I'd held onto like a gummy-fisted child who had the last lollipop. The
scent of his heady aftershave and salty skin made me moan against his
lips.

I was aware of movement and turned my head, catching Alfie slinking
away.

'Stay,' I said.

He raised an eyebrow at me.

'If you want to. I'd like you to.' The vulnerability of my words made
me feel queasy. I'd never put myself in a place to be rejected. I'd never
hoped to be worthy of anyone choosing me.

Alfie looked at Petros, who still had his hands wrapped around my
waist.

'Help us make new memories,' Petros said. 'We all need it.'

Alfie joined us, leaning in to capture my mouth with his devilish
tongue, making me sigh with pleasure. He pulled Petros in, switching to
his lips as I watched them together. It didn't feel dirty or wrong. It felt just
exactly right. Like all of our trauma sent us on a path that was supposed to
converge right there, right then.

Moving behind me, I took Petros mouth as Alfie nipped his way along
my neck. Despite having slaughtered so many monsters, I'd never felt so
powerful as I was sandwiched between them. I'd thought I'd never be
worth one man's adoration, far less two. Even if Alfie's adoration may have
been sexual alone.

Losing myself in their mouths, I felt my top being pulled up over my
head. Then Alfie moved back. Breaking my kiss, I looked over my shoulder
to see him regarding my knotted, scarred back. More a mountain range of
torment than the smooth elegant backs he was likely used to. My cheeks
flamed, and I wanted to snatch back up my top.

'You're fucking magnificent,' Alfie said, moving forward and dragging
his tongue the length of my spine. My brain about fucking melted right out
of my pussy.

Petros reached around and undid my bra, slipping it over my arms
before pulling me up against his chest. 'I've wanted to hold you for so long.
I've dreamt about this moment for as long as I can remember.'

When Petros dipped his head to kiss my neck, before sliding his mouth down my chest and teasing at my nipples, Alfie pressed his mouth against me, his hot breath on my neck.

'Tell us what you want,' he whispered.

The dark little demon bubbled up in my chest, attracted to the promise in his voice. I thrust it back down. 'I can't.

'Do you need it rough?' The way Alfie said it made my knees quake.

I nodded, barely able to admit it to myself, far less to them.

'It's okay to enjoy the darker things in life. It's okay to want both ends of the spectrum. It doesn't make the things that happened to you any less terrible. It doesn't make you fucked-up. Many, many people heal through controlling those experiences and controlling how those actions affect them. You are worthy of love, Harriet. And you are worthy of pleasure. In all its forms.'

I let out a moan. Petros sank to his knees, pulling down the remainder of my clothing and discarding it. His beautiful face looked up at me.

'He can be your light where I am your dark. And I can be his light where you are my dark. Sometimes, one person can be your everything, but other times we fulfil different roles. The three of us need this dichotomy. I will worship Petros with all the fervour with which he worships you. And I will make you squirm in the same ways he makes me squirm. And when you're in the mood, you can turn the tables and unleash it right back on me. Love isn't a finite resource, and neither is pleasure. I've spent my life withholding one while giving the other in abandon.'

Alfie's fist tightened in my hair as he wrapped his other arm tightly around my waist. 'Now you're going to be a good girl and let Petros show you how much he adores you.'

The tight hold on me made me want to fight. And made me wet. My brain struggled with the two until the moment Petros' tongue slid over my clit. Pleasure unfurled inside of me, and I found myself leaning into Alfie's grasp.

'That's it, little monster, spread your thighs so Petros can lap at your pretty cunt.'

I whimpered and did as he said, glancing up at the ornate, red-rosed window above.

'Look at you, spread between the two of us like a needy slut. This is what you've craved, isn't it? Listening to us fuck through the wall while you moaned into your fucking pillow. You thought I didn't know?'

Humiliation filled my cheeks, and I found myself grinding harder on Petros' face.

'I'm going to give your body what it fucking needs, while he gives your soul what it needs.'

'Please,' I whispered, my breath ragged at the divine sensations Petros wrought between my thighs.

'Your safe word is *rose*. Use it if anything I say or do crosses the line from hot to hurt. Understood?' Alfie said.

'Yes.'

A sharp slap against my ass took my breath away. 'Yes, Sir.'

'When we play this game, you play it properly. Otherwise, I'll put you over my goddamned knee and redden your arse properly.'

I heard a zip behind me and practically salivated at the thought of riding his metal-studded dick. 'Do you want a condom, or do you want me to fill you up with my cum like you deserve?'

'I can't get pregnant,' I said. Petros ran his hands up my thighs and squeezed gently. 'They took that too.'

Did my admission ruin the moment? A wave of anxiety swept through me.

'Then you'll take my cum in your cunt like a good little slut.'

Alfie sat back on the pearl-covered table and fitted me over his cock, holding me off him until I began to writhe in desperation.

'Look how beautiful you are,' Petros cooed, slowing his pace to kiss my clit in the most maddening way. 'I could spend weeks kissing every single part of you.'

His words filled me in a different way than Alfie's did. The adoration filled the cracks my trauma had carved into my heart, while Alfie's dirty, degrading words lit a fire in the mended chambers.

'A beautifully needy cock-whore,' Alfie said, using his hands to force my hips down. His cock spread me in the most delicious way, crudely displaying me for Petros.

'Look how well you take his cock, beautiful. Every last inch.' Petros slid his mouth back over my clit before darting his tongue down over the small piece of Alfie's cock remaining visible.

The combo of both a mouth and dick pleasuring me at the same time was mind-blowing. I leaned back against Alfie's chest, our skin slickening between us. He pistoned his cock, each thrust coinciding with a sweep of Petros' tongue.

'Soon enough, we'll fill all your holes, Harriet. Maybe even share your cunt. Can you imagine stretching enough so we could fuck each other inside you? Use your pussy like our own personal Fleshlight.'

A shudder took over my body.

So close.

I reached out and threaded my fingers through Petros' hair, the silken strands giving me enough purchase to ride them both. Alfie slid his hands beneath my knees and spread me wide in his lap. Bouncing me on his cock, he let out a groan.

'Come for us,' Petros moaned against my clit, his tongue lashing at me.

'Show us what a dirty little cunt you are,' Alfie whispered in my ear.

I couldn't fight the sheer bliss that stole through my body. Coming between them sent fireworks behind my eyes. My body juddered and quaked, Alfie gripped my hips painfully hard as he slammed me down onto his thick cock.

'Holy fucking shit,' he groaned in my ear. 'Take every fucking drop.'

And I did.

THIRTY-FOUR

PETROS

Alfie's cum bubbled out of Harriet's cunt with every shuddering plunge of his cock. From my position between her thighs, I got to see every tremor of both of their bodies up close. I looked inside myself, searching for the jealousy that I felt should have been there. Only a desire for more lay beneath the surface. For more pleasure. For more connection. More *love*.

There was no guarantee that Harriet or Alfie would truly want that—that this wasn't just three broken people needing a vacation from their reality for a short time. But I hoped that I could have them both. The woman who I'd spent years trying to put back together using my devotion as glue, and the man who came into my life and knocked me off my feet with his gregarious charm.

Leaning forward, I licked the dripping cum from them, moaning at the combined taste of them.

Alfie groaned while Harriet squirmed in his lap, his spent cock still deep inside of her.

'You're going to stay here until Petros has you good and desperate, and until my cock is ready to take you again. A cock-warmer for us. And after you are begging for us to take you, we will. Both of us at either end of you.' Alfie's voice was clipped, his words faltering every time I swept my mouth from her cum-coated cunt to his balls.

'You taste so fucking good,' I moaned. 'Both of you.'

Harriet's back arched as I sucked her clit into my mouth, grinding my tongue against it. Alfie fitted his hand over her throat, squeezing at the sides. 'That's it, fuck his face for me. Do you feel what you guys are doing to me? Do you feel my cock getting hard inside your wet little cunt? That's how badly we want you, Harriet. We're going to fuck all of that attitude out of you.'

Within a few minutes, Harriet was grinding against my tongue in sheer desperation, her hips rocking as Alfie's cock slipped in and out of her. I sensed the moment she was at her peak, so ready to tip over the edge again, and I stood up, wiping my face.

'Petros, what the fuck? Don't stop!' she pleaded.

Sliding my hands into her hair, I took charge, for once. 'It's time you put that mouth to work, Harriet. It's been empty for far too long.'

Her pupils dilated as I reached down and undid my belt, pulling it off with a snap. My cock was swollen and red-tipped, and I only hoped I wouldn't come the minute she slid her mouth over me. I'd imagined it so many times that my knees were weak with the thought of it finally happening.

'Slowly,' Alfie said into her ear as his fingers slid down to her pussy, replacing the taunting of my mouth. 'Worship his dick. Show him how much you want him to fuck you, and if you suck him off very eagerly, he'll fill you up with another load of hot cum.'

'Yes,' she whimpered, 'I want that.'

'We know you do. You've denied yourself his dick for too many years, you've got a lot of time to make up for. Tongue out, make him feel good.'

The sight of Harriet looking up at me with those big, beautiful eyes of hers was almost too much to take. When she lapped at the engorged head of my cock, I had to steady myself against Alfie's shoulder.

The hot wet strokes were more than just sex. Every single lash of her tongue felt like an apology.

'It's okay,' I whispered, cupping her jaw and stroking a thumb against her cheek. 'Don't be sorry for who you are. I love you like this, but I also love you as you are. The highs and lows. I don't need you to be sorry or to change, just letting me in is enough. *You* are *enough*.'

Her eyes welled up, and she opened her mouth, slipping her lips over my cock and drawing a deep groan from me.

'Fuck, beautiful. I've dreamt of this so many times.'

'So has she,' Alfie said in her ear. 'Haven't you?'

Red filled her wet cheeks as she nodded with a mouthful of cock.

'But you dreamt it would be dirtier, didn't you?' Alfie crooned in her ear while teasing her clit with his fingers. She writhed beneath him, moaning around my shaft.

He put one hand into her hair and hauled her off my dick.

'Tell him,' Alfie demanded.

'I want you to fuck my throat,' she whispered. 'Please, Petros? Fuck my mouth like you've fucked Alfie's.'

Then, Alfie was sliding her back over my cock, roughly pushing her further and further until I slipped deeper into her throat. I couldn't tell if her desperate writhing was from Alfie's fingers on her cunt, his dick inside her, or the lack of breath as I filled her face. It was fucking beautiful.

Alfie guided her head, using her mouth like a weapon. The heat of her gasping throat drove me wild. Seeing her there beneath me, accepting me, wanting me, was a heady rush.

Great strings of saliva connected us even when Alfie pulled her off me, turning her to devour her mouth, giving me a much-needed break. My balls were practically exploding, but I wanted to be inside her. To fill her and mark her as mine, too.

Reaching down, I pulled her off Alfie's cock and dragged her upright, picking her up beneath the thighs and slamming her down on my cock. Her breath caressed my lips with tiny, needy pants.

'Shit, baby, you feel so fucking good. So hot and wet where Alfie's got you ready for me.'

A loud crack made her body stiffen against mine as she let out a cry. Looking over her shoulder, Alfie wielded my belt. 'We're going to make your arse so pretty and red so that Petros has the very best view when he comes inside you.'

I thought she'd use her safe word, that it might be too much. I'd seen her hurt so many times.

'Thank you, Sir,' she moaned, arching her back.

'You're sure this is okay?' I asked against her cheek.

'It's the best night of my life, please take the hurt away with your cock. I need you.'

I shifted inside her, fucking her while standing, and secretly praying Alfie didn't catch my bollocks with the belt.

Every strike of the belt had her writhing on my cock like a demon possessed, her pants and moans hot against my mouth. Alfie and I spoke contrasting words of affirmation, his dirty and degrading, mine filled with love and praise.

'Such a desperate cunt.'

'So fucking beautiful.'

'Beg for his dick like a whore.'

'You're taking me so well.'

When my arms were tired from holding her up, I put her on her knees on the mother-of-pearl table and stood behind her. Her ass gleamed red, stripe after stripe laid across it. I wanted to be repulsed with myself, to tell myself that the fact it looked so fucking hot made me as bad as the others who had hurt her. Alfie came up to my side and dragged his fingers down my spine before kissing me.

'It's okay to give people what they need and want. As long as you are giving them pleasure, and not taking it for your own selfish reasons, it's perfectly fine.'

I kissed him again, glad of his expertise. I'd only seen the bad side of domination and kink. The non-consensual, depraved, sick side. It was rewiring my brain as much as Harriet's to have Alfie walk us through it from a mutually pleasurable standpoint.

'Now let's erase those last horrible memories and give her new ones to focus on.'

Alfie moved to the other side of the table, tipping her head back and kissing her deeply. I slid inside her from behind, the view of them both fucking glorious.

'Time to show us whether you can please us both at once, little monster.' Alfie said, before taking her mouth.

Seeing pleasure glow on his face while hearing her gargle on his pierced dick sent spasms of desire through me. I gave up on the slow, loving strokes after a few minutes and let pure need drive the rhythm of my hips. Alfie met my eyes across her body, lust lidding them as he smiled at me.

Connected.

All three of us.

I wanted the moment to last forever.

Harriet shifted on the table so she could press her fingers against her clit, and it set us off like a set of cum toppling dominoes. She came hard with a desperate cry around Alfie's cock. Neither of us let up our pace. Her cunt strangled my cock, and my vision blurred. Gripping her hips hard, I came deep inside her, riding out every last second of her intense orgasm. Alfie came while holding my gaze, biting his lower lip as he unloaded in the depths of her throat. Our combined moans filled the room, our pleasure wrapping around us like a healing blanket.

She curled up in a ball when we pulled out of her, trembling on the table.

I pulled her up off the table and into my lap on one of the sofas. Alfie fetched a blanket from one of the rooms and joined us beneath it. Tears flowed, and after a few minutes, I didn't know whose tears were whose.

'Thank you,' she whispered, her hand hot against my chest.

'No, thank you,' I said. 'You are fucking magnificent.'

'You really are,' Alfie said, planting soft kisses against her blonde hair.

I wrapped my other arm around Alfie, pulling them both tightly to my chest. It could have been minutes or hours that passed as we lay there in a knackered little pile of limbs. Harriet dozed off in our arms, and I was on the cusp of sleep when Grieves came into the room with a loaded tray of tea and biscuits. I kept my eyes closed as I listened to him talk softly to Alfie.

'They took you, didn't they?'

'Yes, but they had good reason,' Alfie replied.

'Yet here you are, with them both in love with you. How do you do it, my boy?' Grieves' voice was full of pride before he stuttered. 'Sorry, I shouldn't have addressed you like that.'

'I want you to know that I love you. You are the father I never thought I'd have. You are the man who showed me what love could be. I'm sorry that I created space between us to chase after my father's ill-bestowed pride. I don't care about what's proper anymore. You have always been my father in all but name.'

I heard the older man choke up at Alfie's words and smiled to myself as Alfie got up from our little nest and embraced his friend.

He deserved all the love.

THIRTY-FIVE

ALFIE

The wall in the kitchen was littered with photos, notes and other paraphernalia. Pieces of string linked between drawing pins in a huge, tangled web.

Harriet sat scowling at her laptop screen before jotting down scribbled notes and getting up to add them to the wall. I skirted a hand over her hip as she passed me by.

'How's it going?'

She'd practically banished Petros and me for the previous three weeks as she worked day and night on her plan. The three of us were tentatively trying to figure out how to interact with one another in this new normal that Rosenhall had thrown us into. I swear the castle had some sort of ancient magic in it. Maybe the old ladies who talked of the faerie rings in the woods when I was a kid had been onto something.

'Good,' she said, excitement filling her voice. She was thriving with my father's little notebook in her possession. Her eyes glittered. Planning revenge really lit her up. 'I think we can get this show on the road in a couple of days. She stuck the notes alongside a picture of a ruddy-faced man of around sixty. He looked every bit the MP or CEO.

Harriet leant back against me, her back against my chest. I wrapped my arms around her shoulders and inhaled the sweet scent of her shampoo.

'What's the plan? Do we just pick them off one by one?'

'No,' she said, arching her back as I nipped at her throat with my teeth. 'It's too risky. Like birds on a fence, if they see you shoot one, the others will flee. It needs to be a planned strike.

'Tell me how, my beautiful monster.'

'See the one at the top?' I followed her direction back to the ruddy-faced man. 'His name is Hugh Fleming, and he lives alone in a fairly secluded cottage in the Borders. Cottage is an understatement, by the way. It's pretty big. During the week, he tends to rattle about the cottage on his own, only occasionally popping out. But once a month, he invites the other fucknuggets on the list to his home. There's no evidence of what they do there, but I'm doubting very much that they all sit around and play Scrabble.'

Excitement made her words tumble faster, and I couldn't help but smile. Her glee was infectious.

'So, he's the first target?'

'He is. And the bait. He's the one who seems to be controlling the others from what I can see. The one who stepped in to fill your father's shoes. I'm going to make sure he suffers for everything he's done. I remember his face; he enjoyed cutting around the edge of the vaginal entrance so the women would scream all the more as he fucked them.'

'Fucking hell,' I said, staring at the perfectly normal face in the picture. A monster in plain sight. It made my stomach turn.

'So, I get to spend a night torturing him for every single one of the victims he's hurt. He's going to beg me to kill him by the end.'

Her rampant bloodlust should have worried me. Should have made me flee, but instead, I wanted to help her. To join in her fight for all those who couldn't defend themselves. My stabby little heroine.

'You're sure the others will come?'

'Oh yes, he'll tell me exactly how to get them there before I cut out his tongue. We'll have his phone and computer; we'll give them little choice. Blackmail is what keeps the group from turning on each other and self-preservation is a strong force.'

'You've thought of everything,' I said, turning her and planting a kiss right on the end of her nose.

'You and Petros might not want to stay for it all. You might not be able to look at me the same way afterwards.' It was the first hesitation she'd had since we'd come back from Rosenhall.

'We know who you are. All of you. There's no part of yourself you need to hide from us. Plus, you can always fill our heads with pleasant, dirty little images afterwards. There's little an eager tongue can't fix.'

'You're such a slut,' she said with a laugh.

'Takes one to know one,' I retorted.

'Uh, if there's a cuddle fest happening, you two had better make room for me,' Petros said, walking into the room with bags from the burger store. 'Send me out for food so you can canoodle, huh? Which one of you needs the spanking?'

Harriet flushed and squirmed against me.

'There's always room for you, Petros. I've got a lovely little spot right between my thighs...' I winked.

'Okay, you little horn-dogs, first we eat. I'll be pissed if I have to eat a cold burger because you two can't behave for ten minutes.'

Petros sat on one of the bar stools and pulled out his burger, unwrapping it and taking a bite. Harriet looked from him to me before grinning. 'Do you want to have a little fun?'

'Always,' I whispered, grinning back at her.

She pulled me to my knees in front of Petros, reaching up and unzipping his pants. He tried to talk through a mouthful of burger. Harriet held out his dick, and we each took a side, licking and sucking it between us.

'Fucking hell,' he groaned. His cock was rigid in seconds.

'You can keep eating.' Harriet's voice was sultry. 'While we see if we can distract you.'

'Teaming up on me is unfair,' he hissed through his teeth. Harriet slipped her mouth over his cock, taking it deep while I tongued at his balls.

'Do you want us to stop?' I asked.

'Fuck, no.'

We all ate cold burgers for dinner.

THIRTY-SIX

HARRIET

The evening chill brought goosebumps climbing up my arms. I stalked around the rear of the house while Alfie and Petros worked to disable the alarm and the phone lines. Darkness fell upon the house in all but one window. A faint glow came from behind the curtains in the room that I knew was the master bedroom upstairs. The floorplans from the previous sale of the home hadn't been hard to track down in the slightest.

The cottage was old, the sash windows were not even double glazed. No wonder he needed to live so far from his neighbours; there was no stopping any screaming from being heard.

My pocket buzzed, and I snatched up my phone to see the thumbs-up symbol from Petros.

Go time.

A ripple of excitement coursed through me. Using a crowbar, I forced the sash window open. The old wood gave way with little resistance like even the house itself was sick of the monster it contained. Not for much longer.

Dropping the bar, I hoisted myself through the window, dropping quietly into the darkened room on the other side.

The house was deadly silent as I crept to the back door and unlocked it. I didn't wait for the guys. The dark little demon in my core was rising by the second, the urge for revenge making me feel giddy. I could almost smell the decrepit blood coursing through his rotten fucking veins. Begging for me to spill it.

I hadn't bothered with gloves or a ponytail. I didn't intend for there to be as much house left to search by the end.

His grotesque form lay snoring in the large bed, and I took my gun from my waist holster, readying it. My eyes bored into him with each step closer to him. Grunts of air left his slack mouth, drool pooling on his pillow. His podgy cheeks spoke of a likely overindulgence in wine. Fuck, I hoped he didn't have a heart attack and go dying on me. That would be far too kind an end.

'Wakey, wakey,' I barked at him, kicking the edge of the bed while training my gun on his head.

He woke up as slowly as a frog that had been half frozen in winter. It took him a good minute to really register the fact I had a gun pointed at his fat fucking skull.

'Remember me, Hugh? Probably not, it's been a good long while since we last met.'

His eyes narrowed, and he glanced at his bedside table.

'One move and I'll blow your fucking brains all over your pillow.'

'What do you want?'

'What do you think? While I don't doubt you've forgotten who I am over the years, you know I am one of *them*, don't you? You might not remember the way I screamed and begged you to stop because how many hundreds of others have done the same over the nearly twenty fucking years since we last met?' My throat choked up at the thought of others suffering at his hands. The sheer amount of pain one human could cause in a lifetime. Well, here I was to even the motherfucking balance.

Petros burst into the room with Alfie close behind.

'Cuff him to the bed,' I said.

'I can pay you.' Hugh squealed at them. 'I have money. Help me, and I'll triple whatever she's paying you.'

'Oh, sweet, stupid Hugh. I don't pay them anything. We aren't some thugs who've come to extort you. Nothing quite so vulgar.' He struggled meekly as Alfie and Petros cuffed him to the cast iron spindle headboard and footboard. Every thrash of his gelatinous form brought the cuffs crashing into the metal. But he was going nowhere.

Dropping my gun on the bedside table, I climbed on top of him, crushing his chest between my thighs. As much as touching him turned my stomach, I knew that being beneath a woman was degrading to men who enjoyed putting us on our knees; underneath them in every aspect of their lives.

Withdrawing my knife from my pocket, I saw his eyes widen.

'Oh Hugh, what a pickle you've gotten yourself into.'

'Please, I didn't mean any of it. I was forced to do it,' Hugh begged.

'Being forced would be more believable if your dick hadn't been hard, or if you hadn't deployed your knife with so much fucking glee. You're a surgeon, aren't you?'

Hugh paled beneath me and nodded slowly. 'I was.'

'Loved wielding your scalpel so much that you wanted to use it outside of work too... I'd always heard that surgeons had a God complex, and while I'm sure for many it's not true, it's true for you, isn't it?'

'No,' he stuttered.

'Lying won't save you. Do you know how many men I've met just like you? Who think they rule the world because everyone is too fucking afraid to stand up to them. You're not unique. You're a fucking plague. And here I am: pest control.'

I took his hand in mine, threading my fingers between his and twisting, so the back of his cuffed hand faced towards me.

'How many people have suffered under these hands?' I asked, getting close to his face. I laughed as he let out a snarl. With four quick, sharp jabs of my knife, I severed the extensor tendons. His howl of pain made me squirm with joy. I let go of the useless fingers, having removed his ability to straighten them. Taking the other hand, I gave him a sickly-sweet grin.

'Please, not my right hand. I'll do anything. Fuck, please?'

'You've done quite enough.' The second cry was as joy-evoking as the first.

'You know all about tendons, don't you? You made a career out of fixing them.' I got off him and walked down to his ankles. A pool of acrid yellow stained his boxer shorts as I lifted his foot.

'No, please don't.'

'Achilles,' I said. It took a lot more force to cut through the tendons behind his ankles with the way he jerked and fought against my grip. Thank goodness, the cuffs restricted the movement.

'You're making this much messier than it needs to be,' I said through his gasping sobs while wiping my bloodied hands on his bed covers.

I stood above him, watching as tears glazed those red cheeks.

'You're going to suffer terribly before you die, Hugh. But you will die. You and all of your fox-tattooed friends.'

Moving down his body, I found the fading blue tattoo on his thigh. Alfie ducked out of the room. I worked my knife until I'd cut it from his leg, the skin flapping in my hand as he howled. I pushed the bloodied flap between his lips and covered his mouth as he wretched. His eyes bulged, his stomach heaving again and again.

'Swallow it,' I said through gritted teeth. 'This repulsion you feel now, I felt that every time you touched me. Every time you made me bleed just so you could laugh at my tears. This is how you made me feel.'

I pinned his nose with my other hand, watching as his face purpled. At last, his throat bobbed in desperation.

'Good boy.' I smiled at him, patting his cheek as he took great panting breaths.

'You're a sick fuck,' he whispered.

'I am, and you were one of the men who created me. What perfect karma. Now, I think it's time we moved to the kitchen; we've got a little cooking to do.'

Petros stood at the door, looking pale, but still there to support me.

As always.

THIRTY-SEVEN
PETROS

Harriet worked in the kitchen, quietly humming to herself as she did. I watched, somewhat dumbstruck as she grated cheese.

Alfie had gone into the living room with Hugh's phone and computer to begin searching the web for the others. He'd watched a lot less of Harriet's revenge than I had, but this was pushing even my limits.

She picked up a pinch of grated cheese and held it out to me.

'I couldn't,' I said, my stomach churning.

With a shrug, she popped the cheese into her mouth. Hugh was tied to a wooden chair at the dining table, his face a sickly grey.

Boy, he must be having some real regrets right about now.

Harriet raked through his cupboard, beaming as she found the food processor. It still contained the plastic packaging it had come with. Never even been used.

'Well look at that, it's almost as if you bought it just for me. It's a good one too. Nice sharp blades,' she said.

Hugh gave a low moan in the corner.

She bounced over to the large American-style fridge freezer, pulling the door open and taking out the tub of meat. Bowls of chopped onions and garlic, herbs and seasonings littered the countertop where she worked. Plus, her trusty mustard tin of poison.

'Just a quick blitz of the frozen cubes, and it'll mince them right down.' The way the meat landed with small thumps in the food processor made me queasy. The processor jumped to life as Hugh softly sobbed behind me.

Before long, she piled the meat into a bowl and then set two pans on the countertop. Working merrily, she whipped up a bechamel sauce in one while frying the onions and garlic in the other. Adding the meat, the salty, bacon-y smell wafted towards me. It smelled good, and I retched.

Adding the passata, and then the remaining ingredients, she stirred away at the stove. It was a perfectly domestic little horror scene. Picture perfect—if not for the bleeding man in the corner with the severed tendons.

She sprinkled some of the poison into the mixture before scooping a small spoonful out and blowing it. I jumped to my feet, half expecting her to pop it in her mouth.

'Don't worry. Our friend Hugh is going to try it for us. Can't have us feeding subpar lasagne to his friends, can we?' Harriet walked over to him, holding the spoon out like a delighted girlfriend rather than a vengeful aggressor.

Hugh didn't even know about the poison, but he turned his head away, his sobs growing in ferocity.

'Oh, Hugh,' Harriet said, climbing over the growing red puddle pooling on the floor beneath the large hunk of thigh she'd hacked off. 'You've put your flesh in mouths where it didn't belong a hundred times before. What's once more?'

Gripping his hair, she yanked his head back until she had forced his mouth open. She rammed the spoon into his mouth, feeding him his own thigh-based lasagne. Slamming her hand over his mouth, she repeated her actions from upstairs, blocking his nose and mouth until he forced it down.

'How long?' I asked through a choked breath, revulsion prickling my spine.

'Five minutes, if I've measured right.'

She went back to the countertop and started layering the two sauces between the lasagne sheets she'd made at home. Layer by layer, adding mozzarella as she went, it took shape.

Right on cue, Hugh started to cough and splutter so hard that his chair tipped right over.

'Perfect,' she said with a grin.

I collapsed down on the sofa next to Alfie.

The blue computer light reflected against his face, the dark curls of his tattoos creeping up his neck. I wanted to indulge myself in him to free me from the horrors of the kitchen.

'It smells so damn good, right?' Alfie said.

'I don't think I'll be able to eat lasagne again. Ever.' I moved closer to Alfie, pulling him back against my chest and breathing him in. The garlicky meat smell still overpowered.

'Is she okay?' Alfie glanced towards the kitchen where Harriet murmured happily.

'Seems to be. If anything, I'd say she's bloody well thriving.'

Alfie leaned his head back against my shoulder, tipping his face to mine. Reaching up, I swiped his dark hair away from his eyes. A smile ghosted over his lips.

'Do you think it'll really help her?' he asked.

'I hope so. If anyone deserves some peace within their own brain, it's Harriet.'

'Are my ears burning?' Harriet came into the room, smile on her face. She sat across us and wrapped her arms around my neck.

'I hope you've washed your hands really well,' I said, glancing at them.

'Of course. Kitchen etiquette after all. How's the party coming on?'

It still amazed me how easily the three of us fit together. As though I'd been built with two arms solely for the purpose of holding them both. My own little family. The idea of having two people to call my own felt like a pie-in-the-sky idea, but with them both up against my chest, their warmth seeping into me, I had become the luckiest motherfucker on earth.

Sure, we were all fucked-up in our own ways, but who wasn't?

I tuned back into the conversation, grazing my hand over Harriet's back as Alfie filled her in.

'The women will get here around six, and I've briefed them all on what we'll need. They understand the assignment, and I've offered to pay them very well for helping us.'

'You only used people from the list I gave you, right?' Harriet asked.

'Yes, of course, I did, you wee hellion.' Alfie rolled his eyes.

'I didn't believe you were capable of following directions,' Harriet teased.

'Do you think they'll fall for it?' I wondered. 'When they show up, and he's not here?'

'We'll keep them busy with coke, alcohol, and pretty women. They'll be too busy worrying about their dicks to even notice the time. Plus, we have his phone, he'll be updating them the whole time.' Harriet sounded way more confident than I felt. I understood her reasoning for striking them all at once, but they could so easily turn on us with one wrong move.

God, I hoped it worked.

THIRTY-EIGHT

ALFIE

I kept out of view as the men started to arrive. Music pumped throughout the room, scantily-clad women taking coats and giving doe eyes. Apprehension had my palms sweating. It was so fucking risky. Petros had convinced me that Harriet's plans had never failed before.

But neither had they been quite so gargantuan.

The men's faces matched the names as they made their way into the room. It was hard to keep track of them from my place hidden upstairs, peering through the stairs railings in the dark.

John Laurie.

George Lewis.

David Cadbury.

Harry Bowes.

Tom Suttley.

All there. And none had brought anyone with them. Stage one was complete.

Petros looked quite dashing—dressed as a waiter, serving wine to the men.

'Where's Hugh?' a voice asked below.

One of the women draped herself over him, pretending to be halfway to drunk already. 'He's upstairs giving one of the girls a seeing to. She was being ever so mouthy.'

The man grinned. 'Well, that's what happens to naughty lassies, isn't it? I do hope you'll be better behaved.'

'She'll not be able to walk if he's up in her clunge with his bloody scalpels,' another laughed.

I wanted to storm down and shut them up myself. My fingers whitened against the door frame, my breath coming out in a slow hiss. Then, Harriet passed below me, acting every bit the dazzled newcomer. The long ginger wig she wore was a piece of art. If I hadn't known better, I'd have been convinced it was her real hair.

Seeing her touch the men's arms, and throwing pretty, coy smiles their way, sent fiery jealousy burning in the pit of my stomach. I looked down at my core, somewhat surprised. I'd been jealous plenty of times in my life; when my father doted on another child; when the McGowan's had their easy sibling relationships; when I saw couples so wrapped up in one another that it looked like not a single soul in the world mattered but them. Never had I felt it towards a sexual partner. I'd always been more than happy to share.

But Harriet and Petros were *mine*.

The party continued as I watched and waited. Eventually, the men began to grumble, and Hugh's phone lit up with texts.

I responded to only one.

I sent a photo I'd found hidden on Hugh's computer, zoomed in to show the devastation he'd wrought on one poor woman. I could barely look at the horrific image.

Back soon, having too much fun with this cunt. The bitches have dinner for you. Eat, and I'll bring back some dessert.

A phone chimed downstairs, and a heart guffaw followed. 'Sick fuck.'

He reached out the phone and showed the others, some at least having the decency to look somewhat appalled. Right on cue, the smell of the lasagne of doom filtered through the house.

'Damn, that smells good,' one of the men said.

'Sooner we eat, the sooner I can test which of these whores cries the most,' came another voice.

Pieces of absolute shit. Every last one.

THIRTY-NINE

HARRIET

A hand skirted over my thigh, squeezing me hard enough to make me wince. Holding my hand steady, I topped up the man's wine. The urge to crack the bottle over his head was extremely powerful.

No, Harriet. Patience.

The dining room glittered, candlelight dancing across the table, pretty wildflower arrangements beneath the variety of metallic candle sticks. The mantelpiece bore yet more candles, the light in the room low from their orange glow.

Standing up and giving the man a meek little smile, I moved on to the next, topping each glass up. I couldn't help but steal a glance at the impressive floral display hung above the table. It had been a bugger to improvise on such short notice. I only hoped it held up long enough.

Petros placed neatly arranged plates down amongst the glittering silverware. The lasagne looked mouthwatering, oozing mozzarella and a thick, meaty sauce between sheets of fine, thin pasta. On the side, I'd made them a flavour-packed caesar salad and crispy garlic-coated bruschetta. It looked perfectly divine, even if I said so myself.

'Damn, Hugh's missing out,' George, the one who seemed to be most in charge with Hugh absent, said.

He gathered up a forkful of lasagne and stuffed it into his greasy face. Apprehension swirled inside me, and I toyed with a napkin as I waited for his remark. Even chock full of human and poison, I prided myself on my cooking skills. Especially being self-taught for the most part.

'Damn,' he groaned, tucking in with abandon.

The other soon followed suit. Glancing at my watch, I smiled. It was showtime. Alfie should have led the women out to the cars that waited in the woods to spirit them back to the bunker.

I stepped forward and pulled off my wig right as the last fork hit the plate.

'What are you doing? George sneered at me. There was no recognition on his face.

I let down my blonde hair and shook it out about my shoulders, slinking over to the mantlepiece with a smirk. 'What's wrong, you've forgotten me after all these years?'

The men looked at each other, eyebrows creasing. Finally, clarity crossed Tom's face. 'She was one of Rosenhall's bitches.'

Eyes flicked to me with a variety of different emotions crossing their faces.

Fear. Confusion. Anger.

'Where the fuck is Hugh?' George asked, standing up so sharply that his chair flew backwards. Alfie came into the room, giving me a nod saying the others were safely gone.

'He's right here, silly,' I said with a girlish giggle. I severed the wire by the fireplace with a pair of snips I'd hidden behind the candles. A whirring noise rang through the room before the suspended floral board crashed down onto the table. At the same time, I pulled my gun out and trained it on George.

Candles tipped. Glasses smashed. Wine flowed. Hugh's corpse landed smack bang in the middle of the chaos.

'Jesus!'

'Hugh?'

'You twisted little bitch.'

'It's Rosenhall's kid!'

'What the fuck did you do to him?'

'He kindly provided you all with dinner. That delicious lasagne was mostly made from his thigh.' Glee filled me as more than one of them retched. Vomit joined candle wax and wine on the floor.

'You didn't,' said David, the one who was a fucking music teacher. Having such a disgusting prick in charge of youths made me sick.

'Oh, but I did. I cut a great hunk of his thigh while he screamed and begged before making him watch me chop it into tiny chunks. Then I minced it and fried it up so nicely with all of the other ingredients. And now, he's inside of you all. Shame he won't be in there long enough to rot inside you.'

A commotion drew my eyes to the other side of the room. I turned to see one of the men had grabbed Alfie, holding a flick knife to his throat. Petros wasn't close enough to do anything about it, and neither was I.

'Listen, you crazy fucking whore, I don't care what the fuck we did to you, but if you don't let us out of here right now, I'll slit his throat.'

George pushed his seat back as I cocked my gun.

'They can't stop us all. Fuck you lot, I'm out.'

I shot him once, the bullet going through his shoulder and bringing him to his knees, clutching at the wound.

Petros made to tackle the man holding Alfie, but I shook my head at him as he caught my eye. Any second now...

A cough from the table drew my attention. A fresh red splatter of blood coated Hugh's distended stomach. One of the men lunged at me, stumbling in the process. He landed on the carpet at my feet, his mouth moving in a silent plea as blood seeped from his lips. I didn't feel an ounce of pity.

The knife-wielding Alfie-snatcher was bleeding from his eyes, great rivers of red streaming down his cheeks. Alfie turned and pushed him away, the knife clattering to the floor, useless.

'Well, that was close,' Alfie chuckled, the sounds of death rattles and pained begging surrounding us.

'Nah, I had it in hand,' I replied.

Petros looked like he was about ready to pass out. It was like a morbid Last Supper scene. With Hugh a fat, stuffed pig right in the centre of the dying group of abusers. Laughing to myself, I fetched an apple from the kitchen and pulled his mouth open, presenting Hugh like the swine he was.

I dusted my hands off, satisfied with my work.

It wasn't until I went back into the kitchen that a coldness flooded my body, filling in every little part of me that I'd kept controlled for so long.

I'd faced my demons, and I won. They were dead. All the twisted, horrific things they had put me through had been brought up in a judgement day of my very own.

And I'd executed every last one of them.

Not nicely with a bullet through the skull, but with a belly full of their friend and their insides haemorrhaging out of their pathetic fucking faces.

My legs gave way with the enormity of the situation hitting me like a runaway lorry. Cold tiles hit my knees as I dropped to the floor, the pain nothing but a dull ache. Gasping, I tried to inhale, my chest on fire.

A low keening noise filled my ear. It was coming from me. Panic set in as the world closed in around me, my darkness no longer contained inside me as it spluttered out of my face in the form of sobs and snot.

'Harriet!' Petros was on his knees beside me in a moment, wrapping me up in those thick, safe arms. 'You're going to be okay. We're here. We'll always be here.'

More heat hit my other side, Alfie's lips pressing into my hair, his hand caressing my back in slow, relaxing strokes.

'Let it all out, little monster. It's time to let it all go. They don't exist inside you anymore. They don't exist at all. You did it. They can never hurt anyone again.' His words were murmured into my ear as they both rocked me softly in their arms.

'They can never hurt you again. You're ours, and we're yours.' Petros soothed me, neither of them flinching at the sobs which took over my body.

'Plus, at least your lasagne was kick-ass,' Alfie added.

His stupid little comment broke through my pain. I laughed. A deranged laugh that was half hysteria. But it was a start.

Before long, we were all cackling like a pack of hyenas, tears streaming down our faces.

FORTY

ALFIE

Stars glittered high in the sky as I sat on the back step. Not as brightly as they did back at Rosenhall, but few places were quite as secluded as the Highlands.

I stared at my phone.

It seemed to belong to someone else, a stranger who was no longer me. Harriet had given it back to me when we'd returned to the bunker after getting the files, and I must have spent hours staring at the bloody thing. Turning it on meant stepping out of this mad new world and trying to combine it with my old one. After being gone for nearly three months.

But I needed my friends' help.

Nerves rattling around my chest, I pressed the power button. Harriet had kept it charged but in airplane mode, and switched off, and it came back to life with a cheery glow. It felt almost alien in my hands, such a huge part of my life, and yet, I'd not missed the thing at all.

Biting my lip, I closed my eyes.

I knew I could return to the bunker and remain hidden, cosied up in my little love bubble. Grieves would understand. But I wanted my friends too. I needed them. I was done with severing connections and keeping myself apart. Never again.

I clicked the little plane symbol and waited.

Then they poured in.

Notification after notification lit up the screen like it was Hogmanay outside Edinburgh Castle. With it came a level of friendship and love I'd never known had existed for me. From concern to jokes to downright annoyance, people cared. There was even a picture of Ewen and Cora on a mountainside, holding champagne. She looked beautiful in her wedding dress, and he was dashing in his kilt. I'd missed so much. It filled me with joy that even without a word from me, they'd kept reaching out. They hadn't forgotten me.

I pulled up Ewen's name in my contacts and hit dial.

The ringtone went on and on. About ready to give up, Ewen answered breathlessly.

'Alfie?' he said, hesitation in his voice.

'Did I just interrupt a fuckfest?' I asked, grinning.

'Holy fuck, ALFIE!' Ewen practically screamed down the line. 'Where the fuck have you been?'

Joy welled in my throat at the sound of his voice.

'It's a long story, I need some help.'

'Name it,' Ewen said without even pausing for thought.

'Uh, I need one hell of a clean-up crew. Down in the Borders. I'll send you the address.'

'Are we talking sex party clean-up, or dead people?'

Glancing over my shoulder at the cottage, I gave a sigh. 'Definitely the latter.'

'Good fucking Lord,' Ewen said, staring at the scene of absolute destruction in the dining room.

Mac pulled me into a hug, slapping me on the back. 'Missed you. I'm going to need a full run down.'

When he walked past me into the room, he gave a low whistle. 'Holy shit. You did this?'

'Not exactly.'

'Then who did?' Ewen asked.

'Just the most amazing woman I've met.' Harriet and Petros came through from the kitchen, both sets of my loved ones staring at each other doubtfully.

'Harriet, Petros, this is Mac and Ewen. They are kind of brothers to me.'

'We know who they are,' Harriet said, folding her arms over her chest and giving them both a narrowed look. Of course she knew, she'd bloody well stalked me like a little creep.

'Ewen and Mac, this is Petros and Harriet—my dark and my light.'

'You did this?' Ewen asked, walking over to the table and looking at Hugh's grotesquely disfigured form. 'All of this? What was it? Poison?'

Harriet kicked out a hip and eyed Ewen warily. 'I made the pig one into a lasagne and fed it to his friends. But yeah, there was a little poison in there.'

'Christ on a bike,' Ewen muttered.

'You can't talk,' I said to Ewen, 'You put expanding foam up a guy's arse.'

Harriet's face broke into a grin, light filling her eyes. 'Oh, now, there's an idea. I think I'm going to like you.'

'Hey, I needed information,' Ewen said, coolly.

'And *I* really needed all of these fuckers to die.' Harriet shrugged.

'Fair enough,' Ewen ceded.

Mac bumped me with his shoulder. 'So, you're with both of them? Man mountain and the wee psycho?'

'I am.'

'Man, Valentina and Logan are going to be green about the gills.' Mac gave a pleased little chuckle.

Ewen walked around the table, stepping over bodies and sighing occasionally.

'This is too much for us on short notice. I'm going to recommend we call in a friend,' he said at last.

'Who?' I asked.

'Phoenix.'

The man walked in like something from an acid nightmare. Clothed in head-to-toe black, with a full black gas mask covering his face. I'd have thought it only to be safety gear, but it was intricately painted with a phoenix bursting into flame. His heavy boots slowed as he looked over the crime scene.

'Good gravy,' Harriet said, 'he's bigger than Petros.'

'And scarier than you,' I muttered, truly taken aback by the solid figure.

'What do you think?' Ewen asked him.

Phoenix didn't answer, he just turned his masked face to Ewen and gave one definitive nod.

'How long?' Ewen didn't look as intimidated as I definitely felt.

He flashed his hand four times.

'Twenty minutes.' Ewen stated.

One more solid nod before he left the room.

'Where the fuck did you find him?' I whispered to Mac.

'He just kind of cropped up one day. Doesn't speak. Didn't give us a name. Seems happy enough to answer to Phoenix though. You know, because of the mask.'

'What does he do?' Harriet asked, and even she looked a bit perturbed by him. The room almost seemed to ripple around him, like he wasn't fully human. His eyes were almost inky black, like charcoal. His eyes met mine, and it was like my soul went up in smoke.

'He burns shit to the ground. Well. If you want those bodies charred beyond recognition as well as all your evidence up in smoke, he's your guy. Now grab your shit and get out. When it goes up, it's going to be quick.' Ewen was already making for the door.

We gave the house a quick sweep, taking anything of ours with us. Piling out and crunching through the trees. I stopped when an almighty roar blasted through the trees. Within minutes, the trunks were silhouetted orange, the house going up in a tremendous blaze almost unilaterally. Fire normally spreads, but this one all out consumed.

Harriet tugged on my hand, but I couldn't tear my eyes from the inferno. The fire coiled out, licking from within the windows. And then the door opened, and a figure emerged. All in black, walking through the flames like they were nothing. It was a fearsome sight.

He gave me one nod before heading off in the opposite direction.

Who the hell was he?

'Back to ours?' Mac asked, breaking me from my fascination.

I looked at Petros and Harriet. 'Do you want to?'

'Is there a hot shower?' Petros asked.

'And a comfy bed?' Harriet added.

'Both in abundance,' Ewen laughed. 'Not only that, I'll get my wife to order us a fuckload of takeout.'

'No Italian food,' Petros and I said in unison.

FORTY-ONE
HARRIET

Alfie threw his arm over my stomach, his lips idly grazing my shoulder. After a day at the McGowans' mansion, I was glad to have our little trio back in the bunker, alone.

Petros came into the bedroom, carrying a tray laden with coffee, tea, and muffins. His face was more relaxed than I'd ever seen it. Even with the potential repercussions of what we'd done, he looked like a man who'd just taken his first vacation.

Sitting up a little in bed, I grabbed my phone and perused the news. It didn't take long for one headline to jump out at me.

Borders house fire kills six.

'It's happening,' I said. Alfie and Petros curled in next to me and read over my shoulders.

The article mentioned nothing about murder. It stated that the group of friends, all well- connected, older men, had been trapped in their beds as an inferno broke out.

'They're lying,' I whispered. 'Why would they lie?'

Petros laid a hand on my arm and gave me a squeeze. 'It might just be misreported. Or maybe, Phoenix did such a good job of incinerating the place that there was nothing but ashes to go off.'

'No,' Alfie said. 'The press love to sensationalise. It's being quashed. Which is good news for us.'

Relief mingled with anger. Relief that we'd gotten away with it. Anger that those men would be remembered as good family men, or stand-up figures in society. They were the scourge.

'It's not fair,' I muttered. 'It means there are people out there who know. People who know and want to hide it. That can only mean people like them.'

My breaths quickened as I tried to fight the rage and injustice. It wasn't over. It would never be over.

Petros took my phone and placed it on the side, before kneeling over me and planting a soft, searching kiss on my lips.

'You stopped them.'

'Not enough,' I said between kisses.

'Enough for now. There's always tomorrow, my love.' His words soothed me enough to focus on the sweet strokes of his tongue.

'Let us help you forget for a little while,' Alfie whispered, leaning in to kiss my neck, bringing a soft moan tumbling from my mouth.

I gave myself over to them, and let them wash my poisoned mind with their attention. They were like an antidote that could drag me from the darkness long enough to let me catch my breath.

Petros slid down beneath my thighs, and Alfie joined him. Strong hands spread me wide, pinning my thighs to my chest, my oversized T-shirt riding up to expose me to them. I watched with interest as they both angled themselves so that both of their mouths were just there.

I was soaked at the sight of the two men I'd come to adore, both eager to please me at once. My pleasure never felt like a means to an end with them. It was like their sole purpose in life was to bring me to earth-shattering highs.

'Holy fuck,' I said as both of them licked me at once, their tongues sliding and colliding over my clit. Watching them was salacious. Their mouths occasionally clashed for a wet kiss in between lathing me with their tongues. I grasped the duvet in my fists when Petros dipped lower and fucked me with his tongue while Alfie sucked my clit into his mouth. Petros knew well how to inflict devastating pleasure on me, but Alfie was almost superhuman with that damned tongue of his. The coils of pleasure that tore through me with each movement had me begging within a minute.

'I'm going to come. Fuck, don't stop.'

But they did.

With wickedly devious grins on their faces, they turned to each other and decadently took their time kissing.

'You absolute fucking monsters,' I panted.

Alfie reached out without taking his mouth off Petros and shoved two fingers roughly inside me. 'Fuck my hand for me like my good little slut, and we'll give you our mouths.'

Humiliation flushed my face and the effect on me wetted his fingers. When I gave in and moved my hips, Alfie cooed a *good girl* from within Petros' mouth.

Petros reached between them and circled Alfie's hard dick, working the head of his magnificent cock. I wanted it. All of it. Their mouths, their dicks, their attention. I craved it in a way I'd never craved another person. Sex had always been a punishment or a commodity. But with them, it had become an act of worship. A holy trinity of pleasure. I could never get enough.

Alfie fingers splayed inside of me, sending jolts of pleasure into my core.

'What do you think?' Alfie asked Petros.

'I think she needs more fingers.' He slid two of his own fingers along Alfie's, stretching me with them. The intensity made my thighs judder. Their hands slid against each other, both sets of fingers stroking me in different ways inside my pussy.

'Oh my God,' I moaned, falling back onto the pillow and writhing.

'Use your hands to spread that little cunt for us, Harriet. Entice us to feast on it.' Alfie demanded.

The degradation of spreading myself had me right at the edge. When they both dipped their heads and ate like two starving men competing for one dinner, I lost all my mental processing power.

I quaked against the bed, the most ungodly words and sounds ripping from my body like some sort of pleasure-induced exorcism. They didn't let up when the orgasm rocked through me, my thighs trying to close but stuck splayed by the two male bodies between them.

They didn't let up.

Not when the second orgasm washed over me.

Nor when Petros came over my pussy while Alfie licked every drop off.

Not until I'd come so much, I couldn't even talk.

FORTY-TWO

ALFIE

A light breeze made the leaves dance around me.

The scent of summer was heavy in the air, the sweet, perfumey smell of heather, and the piney fragrance of the surrounding woods.

Laughter filled the air, and I looked back towards Rosenhall. An idyllic picture unfolded before me that I'd never truly associated with my home. Grieves was teaching one of the McGowan tots to use a golf club to putt a ball into a cup, her thrilled giggles like birdsong on the air.

Mac lay back on a sun-lounger, Katie curled up between his thighs reading a book. Logan and Valentina walked the tree line, their bodies close. I wondered if they reminisced about their time here, with him hunting her through my woods. Ewen manned the barbecue, arguing with Alec and Cam about the best way to incinerate the sausages. Maeve and Esther sat with Harriet, all drinking cocktails and chatting easily. Even Maeve's growing teens were there, cutting open buns and spreading them with butter.

An arm looped about my waist, and Petros smiled at me. 'You all right?'

'Never better. I can't believe I have all of you.'

'It doesn't surprise me in the slightest. How could anyone resist you?'

His lips drifted over mine, sending that strong, calm vibe of his through me.

'I've lived so many lives here. From being a scared child to being a wild youth to being a love-starved adult. Rosenhall has always been my playground, but it had never really felt like my home.' I turned to face Petros, running a thumb over his cheek. 'Thank you for coming here to live with me.'

'I mean, mansion or smelly old bunker?' he said with a laugh. I gave his shoulder a small shove.

'I'm so fucking happy. I keep waiting for the bubble to burst,' I told him, watching Grieves smiling wider than I'd ever seen him.

'We make our own bubble,' Petros replied. 'If it bursts, we'll just make another. As long as it's the three of us against the world, we can make it work.'

We walked towards the others, and I stopped behind Harriet's chair, sliding a hand onto her shoulder. Her fingers fitted over mine, and she gave me a beaming smile. At times, she was a totally different woman from the one who'd captured me. Relaxed, sweet, affectionate. But when her nest of snakes needed her, she slipped back into her Viper persona without missing a beat. In the months since we'd burned her demons down, she'd wavered about what to do with her life. Nancy had stood up and offered to help. It took a lot for Harriet to hand over any control. Soon she saw that there were other women just like her, who thrived in a space where they could help others. Whether it was to fulfil their need for revenge, or from a burning desire to protect victims, didn't seem to matter.

'Maeve has offered to donate to the cause. They've got Cam's old mansion, where they help put up people who have been abused. It means it'll be easier to house people with nowhere to go. Isn't that amazing?' The way Harriet's eyes sparkled gave me life. I'd do anything to keep them shining.

'It's fantastic, thanks Maeve,' I said, reaching over and ruffling her hair.

'Alfie!' she groaned, trying to smooth her down while laughing. 'You're such a pest.'

'Damn, better hope someone's going to come in and deal with me then,' I quipped with a smirk.

'You're awful,' Esther laughed.

'Awfully good at—' Harriet cut me off, giving me a look that told me to behave myself. I bit my lower lip to stop the smart remark that bubbled at the back of my tongue.

Pulling me down, she whispered softly in my ear. 'Be a good boy, or I'll get my cable ties back out.'

'Oh, little monster. If anyone's being tied down, it'll be you. I know how fucking wet you get when I use your holes and you can't do anything about it.' Her face heated against my cheek as I fought her fire with my own. 'But first, we have a little something for you.'

Petros joined us at the table, carrying a delightful strawberry-covered cake adorned with forty candles. Harriet's face was a picture of shock as everyone gathered around the table, singing *Happy Birthday* at the top of their lungs. Tears pricked at the corners of her eyes as she broke into a smile.

'How did you know? she asked.

'I saw it in your file,' I whispered, dropping my voice low. 'We figured you'd lost enough birthdays.'

Later that evening, Petros, Harriet and I stood on a balcony, looking at the setting sun.

'We got you a little something else,' Petros said, nerves making him jittery.

'You shouldn't have,' she replied, turning to face him.

Petros held out an envelope, not relinquishing it when she tried to take it. 'Please know that this is only an option. You can totally decide what you want to do with it.'

'And please don't lop our balls off,' I added.

Her face was stony as she pulled the letter from the envelope, her fingers tightening over a handful of photographs that were within.

'You found my family?' she whispered, looking up at Petros.

'I looked them up when we escaped together. I thought you might want to go back to them, I wanted to have all the information for you. To make it easier on you. You told me you couldn't go back after all you've been through. I never wanted to go against that, but I kept an eye on them all these years. Just in case.'

Her eyes dipped back to the pictures, a thumb caressing the happy faces within. 'They look so happy. My sisters are so big now, I remember them as teenagers. Are these their children?'

Petros nodded, and her face softened.

'I have nieces and nephews?'

'Quite a few. Your father passed not long after you were taken, I'm so sorry.'

Harriet pursed her lips together, taking in the news. 'And my mum?'

'She still misses you. She never gave up. That letter is from a few weeks ago. She posted it as an open letter to you, wherever you are. I wanted you to see it.'

The letter had made me cry for Harriet and her whole family when Petros had found it. It was the letter that had given him the push to finally bring her family up with her.

'There's a phone number,' Harriet whispered. I handed over my phone. 'What if she doesn't want me? She knew me as a kid, carefree and young. I'm a twisted, broken killer.'

'And she's your mother. That kind of love doesn't diminish if it was there to begin with. It only grows,' I said. 'You don't have to make a decision now though.'

'If I don't do it now, I'm not sure I ever will.' Harriet chewed at her lip as she looked from my phone to the number on the paper.

'Do you want us to go?' Petros asked.

'No. I need you both. Please, stay.'

She moved to one of the sofas, and Petros and I sandwiched either side of her, ready to support her no matter the outcome.

Tension thrummed in the room when the metallic ringing began. A crackle sounded, and then there was a female voice.

'Hello?'

'Mum?' Harriet said, her voice cracking with emotion. There was a pause on the other end, and I glanced at Petros.

'Harriet? Baby? Is that you?'

'It is.' There wasn't a dry eye amongst us as her mum inhaled at the other end of the line.

With the softest of voices, laden with emotion she said, 'Happy Birthday, my darling.'

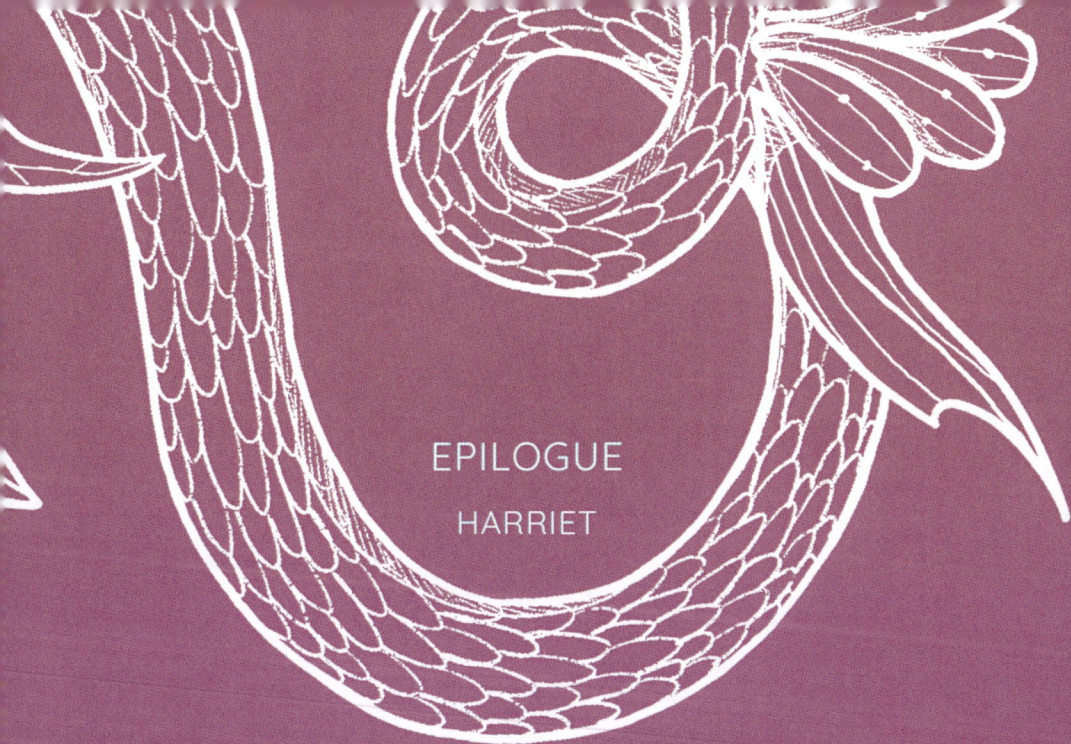

EPILOGUE

HARRIET

Nancy's voice echoed through the tiny, ancient chapel.

Pretty summer blooms decorated the old wooden pews, while white pillar candles flickered on just about every available surface. Despite it being the middle of the day, the private chapel was quite dark, if not for the warm glow the flames provided.

Petros, Alfie and I stood in a perfect little triangle, holding each others' hands. Giddiness filled my tummy as Alfie winked at me. He looked dashing in his kilt and tweed jacket, a sporran hanging around his hips. Petros looked every bit the sharp, sophisticated tux-clad groom.

'I join your spirits together, binding them in an eternal commitment to one another. From this day forth you will go forward no longer as an individual but as a trio. While you will, of course go ahead, celebrating each other's individual accomplishments, you are strongest when you are together. Please all place a hand in the centre, overlapping each other.'

Nancy gave me a sweet smile as I placed my hands atop Petros' and Alfie's.

'These three strips of material resemble each of you. The strip of blue and white—decorated with the Greek key pattern for Petros' homeland. The hem of Harriet's wedding dress—passed down from her mother—

altered to bring in a new love story. And for Alfie? A strip of his family's tartan.'

Nicole moved to stand between Petros and me, draping each of the three materials over our tower of hands.

'May this knot remain tied for as long as love shall last,' she proclaimed, tying a knot in the loose ends of the fabric, pressing our hands together.

'May the vows you speak never grow bitter in your mouths.' I sniffled back tears as I looked from Petros to Alfie, my heart about bursting right out of my chest.

'Hold tightly onto one another through good times and bad and watch as your strength grows. In the joining of hands and the fashion of a knot, so are your lives now bound, one to another.' The third knot sealed the union.

The ancient ritual gave the moment a levity I'd been worried it wouldn't have. Without the legal aspect of our union, I'd thought it might feel empty. But it didn't. It was like all of the people who'd gone before us, who'd tied the knot before there were marriage licenses and government restrictions, came to join us in spirit.

'I love you both so much,' I whispered.

'You too, little monster,' Alfie replied, his fingers flexing beneath my hand.

'Repeat after me,' Nicole said, grinning at us all.

'I vow to love you as long as Scotland flows with whisky.'

Our voices joined in unison as we repeated her words.

'I vow to protect you, and accept your protection, always.'

'I vow to communicate openly to give our union strength.'

'I will love you through the high tides and the low, riding through each ebb together until the day we no longer walk the mortal plains. And, thereafter, I vow to find you, wherever you may be.'

I could barely make it through the sentences, my eyes clouding with tears. Petros sounded as affected as I did, while Alfie spoke confidently, each word punctuated with solemnity.

'I vow that we three shall forever be forged together—hearts, souls, and bodies.'

Alfie raised his eyebrows at the last word and sent all three of us into a fit of laughter.

'You're terrible,' I said.

'You'd both have me no other way.' He grinned at me.

Nancy held the knotted fabric as we slid our hands out.

'Petros, please take Harriet's ring and hold it over her ring finger.' My ring was forged by a local jeweller, a tiny, intricate viper wrapping my finger, clutching a diamond in its jaw.

Alfie moved behind me, wrapping his arms around me.

'We give you this ring as a symbol of our love, like a circle, it has no beginning and no end.'

We repeated the scene with each of the men, taking turns to support and to slide the rings over their fingers. Holding hands with one of my men on either side of me, I beamed.

'With the power that I've absolutely invested in myself, I pronounce you joined together in absolutely unholy matrimony. You can kiss each other silly, now.'

Alfie pulled me in for a slow, tender kiss, his tongue sweeping over my lips until Petros turned my face to his. Our kiss was full of long-awaited joy. I pulled Alfie over, and pressed his mouth to Petros', holding their hands as they sealed our commitment. I felt like I could take on the whole wide world with them at my side.

By the time we'd finished our kiss, Nancy had slipped out of the chapel, leaving us alone.

'I used to hide in here when I was little,' Alfie said. 'And not so little. It was mostly disused, a place where I could come to dream. Never in a million years did I dream I'd be lucky enough for this.'

'Oh Alfie, darling. You deserve every ounce of happiness.' I said, touching his arm.

'You know what else I dreamed about?' he asked, his eyes glinting.

'Does it include your cock?' Petros quipped, tipping his head.

'Always.'

Before I knew what was happening, the men had me sandwiched between them, my wedding dress hiked around my hips as they knelt on either side of me.

I couldn't fight the moans as Petros used his tongue against my clit, driving me wild. Alfie spread my cheeks and set his tongue against my ass, lapping at me. The joint sensation made my thighs quake.

'That's it, Harriet. We need our wife soaked for us because your wedding gift is to take both of us at once, right here in front of the altar.'

'We don't have lube,' I moaned.

'You'd be surprised at what you can keep in a sporran.'

Their mouths worked me up until I was desperate for them; until my body craved them like it needed air.

'Please,' I begged. 'Please fuck me.'

'What do you think?' Petros asked Alfie. 'Do you think we should fuck our pretty wife until we fill her up to bursting?'

The dirty words had me pushing Petros to the ground with my perfect white heel. I climbed on top of him and took what I needed, gasping at the delicious stretch. I barely registered the sound of liquid squirting behind me until cold fingers worked against my asshole.

'I can feel his dick inside you,' Alfie growled, grasping me by the throat from behind. His words were hot in my ear. 'I'm going to fit my cock in your dirty little ass and fuck my husband through your walls.'

'God, yes,' I whimpered, rocking against Petros, his dick sliding in deeper.

Alfie pushed me roughly down, Petros gripping my arms behind my back and pinning me to his chest.

'You've got a whole lifetime of being our beautiful, amazing, cum whore. Look at you, desperate to be used.' Petros' words were ragged against my lips, his dark side finally coming out after months of healing together.

I flinched as the pierced head of Alfie's lubed dick pressed against my ass.

'Fuck,' I groaned.

A hard slap against my ass made me jump. 'You can do better than that. Otherwise, I'll stay right here, just nudging at your slutty little hole.'

'Please? Please fuck my ass.'

Alfie didn't hold back. There was no softness as he pushed his way fully inside me. I came on the spot, the stretch like nothing I'd ever felt before. Alfie's hands gripped my hips like he was holding onto me for dear life. Petros swallowed down my cries, groaning softly at the intensity of them both being inside of me.

The orgasm subsided, and as I panted, they started moving in earnest. Truly fucking each other through the thin wall of flesh that separated their cocks. Sweat gathered at my lower back, their cocks rubbing together inside me. After having an orgasm, the sensation was almost unbearable.

'After we fill you, you're going to put your pretty, lacy panties back on and sit having dinner while dripping us from both of your holes.' Alfie grunted as he spoke, his hips picking up pace as he fucked my ass with rough abandon.

'Touch your cunt for me, darling,' Petros said.

'Yes,' I moaned.

Another sharp smack on my arse had me pushing my hand between Petros and me, rubbing furiously.

'I can't hold off for long,' Petros groaned. Seeing him close made me want to see him fall into lust. I fed off his need like a succubus.

'Almost there,' Alfie groaned. 'Fuck that clit for us, Harriet.'

I did. I tortured the overstimulated flesh until I was brought to the edge again. Alfie's hand pushed into my hair, snatching my head back as he rode my ass like a motherfucking cowboy. It was all the encouragement I needed. My orgasm exploded through me, intensifying with their thick cocks fucking me at a punishing pace. Petros' hands gripped my hips through my wedding dress hard, forcing me down on his cock, while Alfie stiffened behind me, his muscles tensing as he unloaded deep in my ass. I kept rubbing my clit and rocking my hips until we were all utterly spent.

Eventually we collapsed in a pile, Alfie sandwiching me between Petros and he. They didn't pull out.

'That's one way to consummate a marriage,' Alfie sighed, kissing his way down my tattooed back where I'd had the dress lowered to show off my tattoo.

'I think, probably, the very best way,' I giggled.

Taking Alfie had been the best decision we'd ever made.

ABOUT THE AUTHOR

Thank you for reading about Alfie, Petros and Harriet. This is by far the most difficult story I've told, and I hope you enjoyed it.

A huge thank you to my wonderful family. I disappeared for so much time in my office trying to make their story what I imagined it to be. Thank you to Katie, my editor, for keeping me right and sending me hilarious voicemails about the story.

Thank you to you, for reading this book, and to all my readers and supporters. You rock!

Love, Effie

If you'd like to keep up with my books and me, you can find me on TikTok and Instagram (@effiecampbellauthor), Facebook (effiecampbellauthor) and Amazon.

If you enjoyed Alfie, Darling, I'd love a review on Amazon or Goodreads, or wherever you enjoy reviewing books.

Subscribe to my mailing list for new releases and news or join my reader group to chat to like minded smut readers.

ALSO BY EFFIE CAMPBELL

Book 1 - Dark Escapes - Alec and Esther

She's on the run, he's bringing her home. She's not going down without a fight

Book 2 - Dark Enemies - Cam and Maeve

Forced to wed, determined to burn his world down.

Book 3 - Dark Obsessions - Mac and Katie

He's going to save her from her awful relationship, even if it means becoming her masked stalker.

Book 4 - Dark Desires - Logan and Valentina

He's engaged to her cousin, but she knows he's the man for her. She won't stop until he knows it too.

Book 5 - Dark Corruption - Ewen and Cora

She fills in for her twin at the sex club she works at, but she's a virgin. Getting embroiled with her sadistic new boss is a bad idea...

ALSO BY EFFIE

Alfie, Darling

Heart of Wrath

Corrupting Cupid

Theirs for Christmas

Made in the USA
Las Vegas, NV
30 April 2024

89330827R00128